SOPHIE WASHINGTON
LEMONADE DAY

WRITTEN BY
TONYA DUNCAN ELLIS

Other Books by Tonya Duncan Ellis

Sophie Washington: Queen of the Bee

Sophie Washington: The Snitch

Sophie Washington:
Things You Didn't Know About Sophie

Sophie Washington: The Gamer

Sophie Washington: Hurricane

Sophie Washington: Mission: Costa Rica

Sophie Washington: Secret Santa

Sophie Washington: Code One

Sophie Washington: Mismatch

Sophie Washington: My BFF

Sophie Washington: Class Retreat

Contents

CHAPTER 1

The Great Idea

Lemonade (clap, clap, clap)
Crunchy ice (clap, clap, clap)
Sip it once (clap, clap, clap)
Sip it twice (clap, clap, clap)
Lemonade
Crunchy Ice
Sip it once
Sip it twice
Turn around
Touch the ground
Kick your partner out of town!
Freeze!

"Watch out, Sophie!" Chloe yells.

"Whoa!"

I accidentally kick a ginormous, cardboard box off the coffee table before freezing into an Egyptian pose.

My best friend and I are teaching Alexis, the five year-old we're babysitting, a hand game called Lemonade. Back in kindergarten, I was a Lemonade champ. Six years later, not so much.

"Oops!" I squat to pick up the box and tip it over. Papers and file folders spill on the floor.

"Let me help!" Chloe sweeps some of the printouts into a pile with her hands.

"Me too!" Alexis drops her robot pose and slides behind us, tumbling into Chloe. We twist like a pretzel, spreading paperwork all over the rug.

Wiggling near the fireplace, Alexis fans her arms and legs to make a paper snow angel. "This is fun!"

Our spacious den has copy paper everywhere.

"OMG!" I hold my hand over my mouth to cover my giggles.

"Get up, Alexis!" Chloe snickers, scooting to us on her bottom, and one of the papers rips.

"Girls!" Mom rushes into the room, and we freeze for real. "What are you doing?! I spent two hours organizing these files!"

My stomach drops.

Mom just started her own consulting company, where she gives advice to people starting their own businesses. And already, I'm messing it up.

My mother's main job is helping out in Dad's dentist office and taking care of me and my eight-year-old brother, Cole. But before she got married and had us, she worked at a bank. Now that we're getting older, Mom wants to start working on her own again. This new consulting business is her chance.

"I'm sorry, Mom." I wring my hands when she crosses her arms around her chest. "We didn't mean to wreck your work. I'll fix these."

I set some files on the table, not sure what order they go in. Paper crinkles as Alexis imitates what I'm doing and mixes things up even more.

Mom rushes over to stop her.

"Why don't you girls sit on the couch?"

My mother is meeting with Alexis' mother, Mrs. Gentry, to talk about ways to sell more of the scented candles she makes. Since Mrs. Gentry couldn't find a babysitter for Alexis she asked me and Chloe to keep an eye on her.

Mom made the big announcement about her consulting company at dinner last week.

"I know so many women with great business ideas who aren't sure how to get started," she explained to my father. "I want to help them get bank financing so they can be successful."

"Is that like *Shark Tank?*" asked Cole.

"Sort of." Mom smiled and rubbed his afro.

"What's *Shark Tank?*" I asked.

"That television show where people try to get investors to pay for their business ideas," Dad explained. "We watched it when you had a sleepover with your friends last weekend."

It's a good thing that my father took my brother to his basketball practice this morning. If Cole saw this mess in the family room, I'm sure he'd have jokes.

I'll admit, the one he told at breakfast this morning made me laugh.

"What's a nosy pepper do?" he read from his joke book. "Get jalapeno business!"

Distracted by my thoughts, I hop up from the couch to try to clean up again and slip on a piece of paper.

"You know what? How about you girls go play outside?" Mom shakes her head. "I'll take care of this."

4

She stacks some piles on the coffee table.

"Is everything alright?" Mrs. Gentry comes from the kitchen.

"Sophie and Chloe taught me how to play Lemonade!" Alexis claps her hands and rocks, so that her brown ponytail bobs.

"The kids are getting antsy in here." Mom shifts her eyes to the door.

"Come on, guys. Let's go." I lead the other two girls to the backyard.

As we open the gate, I feel like my dog Bertram does when he's caught chewing Dad's shoes.

"Sorry for getting you in trouble," says Chloe.

"Me too." echoes Alexis. "Yay! A puppy!"

Bertram bounds toward us, and she chases him around the yard.

Our black, Portuguese water dog is in doggy heaven as we throw him a tennis ball and scratch his curly fur.

<<<<<<<<<<<◇>>>>>>>>>>

Forty minutes later, Mom calls us back in. A caramel scented candle has our kitchen smelling like a bakery, and she's smiling. I guess the rest of the meeting went well.

"Here's a snack, girls." She sets a plate of cookies on the table. "I'm sure you're hungry after all that running and jumping."

"I'm really excited about all your suggestions." Mrs. Gentry walks in from the restroom. "The marketing ideas are fabulous. I'm glad you're setting things up so I can sell my candles on the Internet. I'd been happy getting a booth at the Farmer's Market every Saturday, but I know I need to grow. I can't wait to see the business plan you put together. Thanks for taking time with me."

She turns to Alexis. "Did you have a good time with Sophie and Chloe? I hope she wasn't too much trouble."

"None at all, Mrs. Gentry," answers Chloe. "It was fun."

"Yeah, we got to play lots of games we liked in kindergarten, without feeling babyish." I nod.

"I love Sophie's puppy!" says Alexis. "Can we get one, Mom?"

"Taking care of dogs can be expensive. We'll have to see how my business does," says Mrs. Gentry with a chuckle.

She grabs Alexis' hand and moves toward the front door. "Let's meet again next week. You can definitely sign me on as your first customer."

"Oh, and here's a little something for you and Chloe for helping me out." She hands us both five dollars.

"Thank you, Mrs. Gentry!" We say at the same time.

"It's so cool that your mom's helping Mrs. Gentry sell her candles," says Chloe a few minutes later in the den. She scrolls through her phone, and I half-watch a cartoon on the flat screen over the fireplace.

All the papers are picked up, and the room's back the way it usually looks, with bright, comfy throw blankets on the soft, leather couch, and the colorful, wool rug brightening the tile floor.

Over in the kitchen, Mom's on a call with Dad, telling him the good news about her first customer.

"We should start a business," says Chloe. "It'd be cool to make our own money. I want to get some new leggings at the mall, but Mom says they cost too much. If we had our own business, I could save up and buy them myself."

Even though we wear uniforms at Xavier, the private middle school where we're sixth graders, Chloe keeps up with all the latest fashion trends. She saved her allowance for six months to buy the red canvas shoes she's wearing today. With her long legs and shiny, black curls, I wouldn't be surprised if she becomes a fashion model when she grows up.

"I'd like to make some extra money, too," I say. "Mom's birthday is coming up, and I'm saving to buy her a pretty bracelet I saw at the jewelry store. But what would we sell in our business? I've seen Mrs. Gentry make candles, and that looks hard. And Mom says I can't babysit on my own outside the house until I'm twelve."

"I know!" Chloe passes her phone over to me. "Lemonade!"

A cartoon lemon with arms and legs standing behind a pitcher of lemonade smiles on the screen.

"You mean have our own lemonade stand?"

"Exactly! Our school's doing Lemonade Day this year!" exclaims Chloe. "We should sign up!"

CHAPTER 2

Lemonade Day

"What's Lemonade Day?" I tap on the video on Chloe's phone to get more information.

A map of the United States with lemonade stands overlaid on it pops up. "Wow! It's nationwide." I exclaim. "I remember them talking about this over the announcements during homeroom the other week, but I wasn't paying attention."

"Neat, isn't it?" agrees Chloe. "It says here that Lemonade Day started with two thousand kids, and now there are over a million. And it began right here in Houston. They teach you how to start your own business and make tons of money!"

"How do we join?" I look over her shoulder after she takes her phone back.

"At school on Monday before homeroom," she answers. "Lucky we noticed it, because that's the cut-off time for sign-ups. We have to have a mentor teach us the steps to start and run our own business. We can get a teacher to mentor us, or choose someone else. There's judging, and there can be up to five people in our group."

"What group?" asks Cole as he and Dad step through the back door. Bertram wags his tail behind them. In his blue and gold uniform and knee socks, my brother looks like a mini-NBA player. To top off his outfit, he wears a gold sweatband and a blue arm sleeve.

"You back already?" I sit up straight. "I thought you were on the phone with Mom."

"We were pulling up into the subdivision when she called me." Dad sits a box of donuts on the counter.

"Here you go with the sweets again," Mom says and kisses Dad on the cheek. "You'd think as a dentist you'd want to limit these kids' sugar."

"I know." Dad shakes his head. "But I saw the line at the donut shop on the way home and couldn't resist."

The sight of sweet treats draws me and Chloe to the kitchen. We sit down on tall stools that line the dark granite-topped island and grab a couple to snack on.

Like the rest of the house, our kitchen is super organized. The gray counters are empty of clutter, except for the coffee pot and a cook book on a fancy stand. Mom believes in a place for everything and everything in its place. "Get that dog out of here!" She fusses as Bertram whines. Mom gets irritated with him when he begs or chews up something, but sometimes when she cooks, she sneaks him bites of food. When he followed us home a few months ago we thought we couldn't keep Bertram because Mom has fur allergies. But since he's hypo-allergenic, being around him doesn't make her sneeze.

"Sophie, can you please get some of your old sneakers and boots off the shoe racks in the laundry room after Chloe leaves?" Mom asks. "I want to store all our shoes in there to keep them away from the dog. How'd you do in the game?" she asks Cole, after shooing Bertram outside.

"We won by five points!" Cole holds his hand in the air and imitates a shooting motion. "I wish you could've been there. I made two three-pointers."

"Sorry to miss it." Mom pats his back. "I'll try not to schedule any more meetings on game days."

"I'm proud of you for being so dedicated to your business." Dad gives her a side hug. "You're already on your way to success."

"Chloe and I are starting a business too." I announce. "Our own lemonade stand!"

Dad looks at us questioningly.

"Our school's having Lemonade Day to teach us about entrepreneurship," Chloe explains after finishing her donut.

"Would you be our mentor, Mom? We need someone to help us…" I pick up Chloe's phone and start reading, "…create a budget, set profit-making goals, serve customers, repay investors, and give back to the community."

"That sounds like quite the undertaking." Mom sets her coffee cup on the table. "By when would you need to do all this?"

"In two weeks," says Chloe. "That's the actual Lemonade Day. Kids all over the city will be selling lemonade. Our mentor has to teach us the steps we need to start and run our own business."

"I want to help with the lemonade stand too!" Cole bounces on his toes.

"I don't know about this." Dad folds his arms across his chest. "Your mother is going to be busy the next couple of weeks getting her own business off the ground."

"This may be a way for me to teach the kids about entrepreneurship," says Mom. "I'd love for them to become business owners one day. I'll help you girls with your lemonade stand. Sounds like a great idea!"

"Can I help?" Cole whines. "I can make lemonade."

"Can't he do something with *his* friends?" I frown. Cole is always butting in with what I'm trying to do. "He can make his own lemonade stand."

"Asking your mom to mentor two different Lemonade Day groups is a bit much, Sophie." Dad shakes his head. "It wouldn't hurt you to include you little brother in your business. It could teach you some teamwork skills."

"I don't mind if Cole's on our team." Chloe pats his head, and he grins like he's won a prize at the carnival. Cole says girls are yucky, but he lights up like a Christmas tree whenever my best friend is around. She has that effect on most of the boys in our sixth-grade class too. With her big black eyes and dimples, it's not hard to understand why. She's as nice as she is pretty, which is why we've been BFFs since kindergarten.

"There aren't age restrictions on the teams, Sophie." Mom scrolls through her phone for more information. "I don't see any harm in including your brother."

"Okay." I shrug my shoulders. "But you better not embarrass me at our lemonade stand, Cole."

"Ahhhh!"

He shrieks and does a crazy, victory dance around the kitchen, proving my point.

"Get more information about Lemonade Day at school on Monday, and we'll go from there," Mom says.

"Great! We'll see if we can add two other kids to our team too," says Chloe. "It'd be good if we could have a full group of five to split up the work."

We brainstorm ideas for how we can run our Lemonade Day stand until her parents come to pick her up.

"Let's paint our stand a pretty color! Like yellow!" suggests Chloe.

"We could add a vase with sunflowers for decoration," I say.

When Chloe leaves, I read over all the information again, to make sure I understand what to do. *This is going to be so much fun!*

CHAPTER 3

Sign-Ups

Finding two other people to be in our group isn't easy.

"My grandparents are visiting from Africa then." Our friend Mariama looks at the Lemonade Day date and shakes her head. "Since this is their first trip to Houston, we're taking them on a tour around the city."

Mariama's family is from Nigeria. Chloe and I became close with her during spirit week last year when we dressed as African queens. We won first place on one of the spirit days, wearing the colorful gowns and head wraps Mariama's mom made us.

"Ah man! That's playoff week," announces Toby, when we flag him down. "Coach told us to leave that date open to do some extra workouts. If you have anything else going on, on another date, let me know. It's always fun working with you girls." He flashes a bright smile before running to the gym, and I blush.

We're at our normal meeting spot by our lockers before homeroom. Kids surround us on each side of the hallway, socializing and getting their books and materials for class.

"Sorry, but I can't do it either," adds Valentina, captain of our cheer team. "My cousin's quinceañera is on that day. No way can I miss that."

"What's a quinceañera?" I ask.

"Sort of like a Mexican sweet sixteen party," Valentina explains. "Quince means fifteen, and girls have a quinceañera when they turn fifteen years old. It's a coming-of-age ceremony, showing that the birthday girl is becoming a grown-up. The court wears ball gowns and tuxes, like at a wedding, and we have a church ceremony beforehand. It's a really big deal."

"Wow! That sounds beautiful, Valentina!" Chloe looks starry-eyed. "Will you have a quinceañera one day?"

"I hope so, and I want you guys to be in my court!" Valentina smiles at us.

When I first met Valentina, I was jealous of her. Her long black hair hangs down her back perfectly like she just left the hair salon. She's great at gymnastics, and everybody follows her around like she's a celebrity. I thought she was fake. But once I got to know her better, I found out she's really cool.

"Excuse me!" Carly. another one of the sixth graders, steps between us with a stack of fliers in her hands. "I need to hang these up here."

She attaches a blue printout with a picture of dogs and cats on it onto a nearby wall.

"What's that all about?" asks Mariama.

"I'm raising money for the animal shelter where I volunteer," Carly answers. "Money from donations helps them stay open and be able to rescue more animals."

15

"That's really nice!" I say.

"We need to make sure all these animals are placed in loving homes," she explains. "If the shelter doesn't get enough money, some of them may be put to sleep."

Carly is a true animal lover and says she wants to be a vet one day.

"Hey, Carly, want to join our Lemonade Day team?" I ask. "The Lemonade Day rules say we have to donate some of the money we earn to charity. How about giving part of it to the animal shelter, Chloe?"

"That's a great idea!" Chloe clasps her hands. "Good thinking."

"What would I have to do?" asks Carly.

"Help us put together a business plan and run our business," I explain. "On Lemonade Day, we put all that we learn to use and earn money at our very own lemonade stand. Lemonade Day is two weeks from now."

"How much money do you think we can make?" Carly asks.

"Two hundred dollars, at least," I say. "The fliers say the average team makes about one hundred sixty-eight dollars in profit, but I'll bet we can do better than that."

"We have to get someone to sponsor our stand too," says Chloe, "So we'll need your help with that. Can you meet after school on the playground?"

"I'll do it! Thanks for asking me!" says Carly. "Anything to help the animals. I need to get the rest of these fliers up before homeroom. Talk to you later!"

"One down, one to go." Chloe looks around for our next possible team member.

"Excuse me! Coming through!" Nathan Jones, our class brainiac, nearly stumbles into us.

He's holding something that looks like a square-shaped toy gun in one hand and a big poster board with equations written on it on the other.

"Where you headed to, Nathan?" I step in his path to slow him down.

"Just dropping this off to the science lab before homeroom," he answers. "I'm working on an extra experiment on velocity after school."

"What's velocity mean?" I ask. "And what's that thing in your hand?"

"Velocity means speed. And this is a radar gun; I'm using it to measure how fast our laboratory rats run under different conditions."

"Have you heard of Lemonade Day, Nathan?" I show him the flier on my cell phone. "It's a fun project where you start your own business."

"And help charity too!" Chloe adds.

"The big event is coming up soon, and we'd love for you to be on our team." I hold my phone out to show the information.

"Sounds interesting." He peers down at the screen over his dark-rimmed glasses.

"We have four others on our team and need one more person," I add. "We have to come up with a financial plan for the business, which uses lots of math, and I think you'd be great at that!"

"I see the project needs an investor too." He runs his finger down the screen. "Maybe my dad could donate some money."

Nathan's family owns a Fun-Plex arcade center, where lots of kids from our school have birthday parties. His dad makes him work at the center after school sometimes, and nearly every weekend. My favorite thing to do there is ride the bumper cars.

"I think I can do it!" says Nathan.

"Our Lemonade Day team is going to rock!" Chloe does a happy dance, and I give her a high-five.

"This is so cool!" I exclaim. "With you on our team, we might even have a chance to win!"

"Wait a minute, what date did you say it was on again?" Nathan pulls a calendar out of his pants pocket. "I forgot, the science competition I'm entering is that Saturday. My bad."

My stomach drops.

"You sure you can't help us, Nathan?" I plead. "We really need you."

"Sorry, guys, but I've been getting ready for this science event for weeks." Nathan puts his hands in his pockets. "My dad would blow a gasket if I dropped out to sell lemonade."

"Thanks a lot for getting our hopes up!" I pout and wrap my arms around my chest.

"Aw, don't get mad, Sophie," says Nathan. "You know I don't want to let you down."

The first warning bell rings.

"Come on, girl, we'd better sign up for Lemonade Day before it's too late." Chloe tugs on my arm. "It'd be better if we have five people, but four will be okay. See you later, Nathan!"

"See ya! Sorry again, guys."

I cut my eyes at Nathan one last time before we speed-walk to the principal's office.

CHAPTER 4

Game Plan

Chloe and I make it to the principal's office to sign our team up for Lemonade Day just in time.

"I was getting ready to take down the sign-up list," says Mrs. Jenkins, the school secretary. "They're limiting it to just ten Lemonade Day teams this year, and you're our last one. The other groups have already been working for a couple of weeks, so you'll need to play catch-up."

She makes a mark in her notepad. "Let's put your booth in section number ten."

"Thank you!" I say, neatly writing our team members' names down on the sheet.

We have our first meeting after school.

"Let's give everyone a job." I pull printouts with information about Lemonade Day from my backpack and hand them to Chloe and Carly.

We're gathered at a picnic table beside our school's playground for our first official team meeting. As usual in Texas, it's humid. I slide off my cardigan sweater to get comfortable.

Mom's working late at Dad's office most days this week, so she said she'd start mentoring us after school on Thursday. We're still waiting for Cole to walk over from the elementary wing. Kids scramble around us like ants.

"Where is that boy?" I complain to the other girls. "We're already at a disadvantage since Nathan bailed on us. We need to get started."

Xavier's playground is in an indoor courtyard area in the middle of the school. Fifth-graders play kickball on crayon-green artificial grass. Off to the side, some smaller kids pump their legs on swings, while others swish down the sliding board. Motion on the monkey bars catches my eye.

"Is that Cole?" Chloe points in that direction.

Upside down by his knees, with his shirt untucked, he struggles to pull his polo out of his eyes.

"Your brother is too much!" Carly giggles as he wiggles around like a fish. I swear his goal in life is to embarrass me.

"Cole Washington! You get over here!" I cup my hands around my mouth like a megaphone.

One of his legs slips off the silver pole. "Whoa!"

"Oh no!" I cry.

Cole thuds to the ground. For a second, I freeze.

Around us, other kids and the playground monitor keep playing and talking, not noticing what just happened.

"Cole! Are you alright?!" yells Chloe.

I snap to, and we all run over. My brother lies still, his eyes closed.

"Is he breathing?" I put my fingers on his wrist to check his pulse like they do on TV medical shows.

My chest tightens, and I blink back tears. I get ready to call for help, and then Cole pops up like a jack-in-the-box.

"Tricked ya!" he sing-songs and then laughs.

"That isn't even funny, Cole!" I hit him on the back, once he's fully standing. "I was scared you broke your neck."

"I'm not a scaredy-cat like you, Sophie." He flexes his muscles. "I'm strong."

"Whew! That was too much." Chloe shakes her head and snickers. "You sure had us fooled."

"Come over here, silly, so we can get to work." I pull his shirt sleeve and walk back to the picnic table.

I'm already wound-up since we only have four, make that three-and-half counting Cole, Lemonade Day team members.

"I'm hungry, Sophie." He wiggles in his seat as soon as we sit down. "Got any snacks?"

"Just chill." I shake my head. "We won't be here long."

"Do you like sunflower seeds?" Carly reaches in her backpack. "I always keep some for emergencies."

Cole bites into one, makes a face, and then spits it out on the table.

"You're so rude!" I pull a tissue out of my bag to wipe up the seed. "Don't make a mess with that."

"But it was nasty!" He pokes out his lip.

I sigh. "Keep it up, and I'm taking you to the library for aftercare until Mom comes."

Ignoring me, Cole pulls out a piece of paper and a pencil from his folder and starts sketching something. Happy he's quiet, I leave him alone.

"While we're here, we need to take care of five things." I gesture with my fingers. "A business plan, sponsorship, operations, marketing, and charity."

"I don't know what any of that stuff means," mutters Cole as he continues doodling.

I cross my arms. "That's why we should have had another sixth-grader on the team and not a baby."

"I'm not sure about all those things either," says Carly. "Can we review them before we get started?"

"Sure," I sift through my stack of papers and jerk when Nathan rushes to the table. His glasses almost slide off his nose as he plops in an empty chair and drops his book bag beside it.

"Cole! My man! How're you doing?" Nathan high-fives my little brother. "Didn't know you were on the team. Hope I didn't miss too much!"

"You're doing Lemonade Day?" I wrinkle my brow. "I thought you had your science project."

"If you still need me," he answers. "The science teacher says I can do my presentation the weekend after Lemonade Day."

"Yay!" Chloe raises her hands in the air like we do at cheer practice. "We definitely want you on the team, Nathan."

I feel like I've set down a heavy backpack.

"You made it just in time, Nathan!" I talk fast so he can't back out. "I was getting ready to go over everybody's jobs on our team. For Lemonade Day, we've got to come up with five things: A business plan, or outline of everything. A sponsor to give us money for supplies. Operations, or making of the actual lemonade, and our lemonade booth. Then we do marketing to tell people what we sell. And last, but not least, is charity, meaning, who we'll donate some of our sales money to."

"Wow, Sophie!" Chloe bugs her eyes. "You sound like a real business woman."

"She ought to," says Cole. "She stayed up past her bedtime reading the information."

"I'll ask my dad to sponsor us," says Nathan, "I'm sure he'll agree to loan us money for supplies. And I can help put together and type the business plan too."

"Sounds great!" Chloe gives the thumbs up sign. "That's two major things taken care of."

"I want to do operations." I raise my hand. "My grandma makes a yummy lemonade recipe with berries in it we could use. And I'm sure my dad will help us build our lemonade stand."

"Can I help decorate the stand?" asks Chloe. "I love doing design."

"And I'll be over charity, of course," says Carly. "Maybe we can display pictures of some of the animals on our lemonade stand, or even bring them. I'll ask the shelter director. It'd be wonderful if we could find some of them homes!"

I glance over at Cole and frown. He's still scribbling, while we're coming up with great ideas. I knew we shouldn't have let him on our team.

"And what are you going to do while everyone else is working, Cole?" I ask. "Draw?"

He's so into what he's doing that he doesn't hear me.

"Look at that!" Nathan points at Cole's sketch pad.

As we've been talking, my brother has drawn a picture of a girl with two braids at a lemonade stand and a dog beside it.

"That's super cute, Cole!" says Carly. "That girl looks just like you, Sophie!"

"Cole's won blue ribbons for his art at the Houston Rodeo," says Chloe. "He's the perfect person to do marketing for our team! We can use this design for posters to advertise our lemonade stand."

"Yeah, that's a great idea!" says Nathan.

"Thanks!" Cole leans back in his chair, grinning like a smiley-face emoji.

Studying the awesome picture, I feel silly for fussing at my little brother. I've got to make sure my lemonade tastes as good as his artwork looks.

"Can we finish up for today?" Chloe looks down at her cell phone. "My mom just texted that she's in the carpool line to pick me up."

"Our mom will be here soon, too," I answer. "Let's plan to meet at our house on Thursday. Mom can drive us all there after school. She said your parents need to pick you guys up from our house by five."

"Thanks, guys." Carly stands and grabs her backpack. "I'm so excited about Lemonade Day!"

"Me too," says Nathan. "We're gonna do great!"

"Come on, Cole." I help my little brother get his things together. "Let's go to the carpool line."

CHAPTER 5

The Berry Special

In the carpool line, I tell Mom how the first Lemonade Day meeting went, and she's impressed. "Way to take charge!"

"We were nervous we couldn't get anyone to join our team," I start. "But everything worked out. Chloe…."

"Look at this, Mom!" From the backseat, Cole holds up his drawing, interrupting me.

"Amazing! I love the details." Mom acts like he's a junior Picasso. "Let me get a closer look." She peers at the paper. "Wow! That girl behind the lemonade stand looks just like your sister!"

As she drives the car out of the parking lot, my mother goes on and on about Cole's picture. Forget how I organized everything and let him be in our group in the first place. I scoot closer to the passenger side window, quiet. He always steals Mom's attention.

When we pull up to the driveway of our two-story house, her cell phone rings.

"Hi, honey! How's it going? You *have* to see the drawing Cole did at the kids' Lemonade Day meeting today! Here Cole, let me take a picture to send to your dad."

While she brags to my father about how great Cole is, Mom presses the garage door opener. Neither she nor Cole notice when I leave the car and punch the keypad code to get inside.

"Hi ya, boy!" I talk in a baby voice to Bertram. He wags his tail and tries to jump on my knees. At least someone is happy to see me.

"Who wants a snack?" Mom asks when she and Cole come in a couple of minutes later.

"Me! Me! Me!" Cole bounces up and down. Sensing that food is on the way, Bertram rubs against his leg.

"I'm really excited about this Lemonade Day project you kids are doing," says Mom as she puts cheese and crackers and celery sticks on a plate for us to munch on. "You should learn a lot and have fun."

"Yeah, it'll be okay," I answer, flipping through my science book like I'm busy. *Now* she wants to talk.

"Guess what happened in my class?" asks Cole, and Mom forgets I'm here again.

"Drew Jenkins waited too long to ask for the bathroom pass and peed his pants!"

"That poor boy! I hope the kids didn't tease him too badly," says Mom.

"They shouldn't have," I say. "They're all babies."

"Now, Sophie, that's not nice." Mom shakes her head.

I pout and pull out my homework folder. While I start on a vocabulary sheet, Bertram sits at my feet with his head on his paws. Usually, we take him for a walk as soon as we get home, so he's probably disappointed.

Cole pulls out his joke book to read. Unlike me, he hardly has any studying to do after school. He'll be shocked when he hits sixth grade and gets assigned loads of homework every night.

"What's the sign outside the pet store say?" He bursts out. "Buy one dog, get one flea."

"Can you be quiet?" I fill in an answer on my worksheet. "I can't concentrate."

"Sorry, Sophie," he answers. "Just trying to make you laugh."

I frown.

Near the stove, Mom layers strips of tortillas in a casserole dish and adds a mixture of shredded chicken, cream of chicken soup, diced tomatoes, onions, peppers, and cheese. My mouth waters. I love her King Ranch chicken.

"I need to drop something off at Mrs. Gentry's. Anyone want to join me?" Mom pushes buttons on the oven panel.

"I'm finishing my homework." I answer.

"I'll come!" Cole sets down his book. Mom grabs her briefcase near the door.

"See you in about an hour, sweetie." She waves before they step out to the garage. "If your father gets home before we do, tell him dinner should be done shortly. The casserole's in the oven on a timer, so it'll turn off by itself. Oh, and when you get a chance, can you clear some of your shoes off the rack in the laundry room? I don't want to leave them in the garage anymore because Bertram might be tempted to chew them."

"Okay, see you later!" I say and turn back to my vocabulary worksheet. Ten minutes later, I finish quicker than I thought I would.

Now's my chance to try to make Granny Washington's famous lemonade recipe without Cole underfoot. I want it to be really good, so Mom and Dad can see what a great Lemonade Day team member I am. Maybe we can serve it with our dinner tonight!

"Let's see, what does Granny put in her lemonade?" I tap my fingers on my chin. I could call her up to ask, but I want to do it myself.

My grandmother makes two types of lemonade. Regular, with just lemons, and another one she calls the "Berry Special" with strawberries and blueberries in it. The Berry Special is Dad's favorite, but since it's my first-time making lemonade, I'll stick with the plain kind.

I open the refrigerator and grab six lemons from the bottom drawer. Then I pour some water in a sauce pan, and turn the stove on to get it boiling.

Mom doesn't like me cooking without her home, but since it's for business, I don't think she'll mind.

While the water's warming, I check in the pantry for sugar. Great! Mom already has some poured in a measuring cup, so I don't have to worry about spilling anything. I dump it in the pan.

I slice the lemons and squeeze the juice in a glass pitcher, getting the seeds out with a small spoon. Granny always leaves in the pulp because she says it gives the lemonade "extra oomph."

I'm so focused on what I'm doing that I don't notice Dad come in through the back door.

"You making dinner?" he asks.

My stomach growls from the cheesy scent of the heating casserole.

"Just lemonade," I answer. "Mom and Cole are at Mrs. Gentry's."

"It smells great in here." He sorts through some envelopes on the counter. "Hope they get back soon, so we can eat."

"Mmmm…mmmm…mmmm." Bertram whimpers in agreement.

The water has been boiling for a few minutes, so I turn off the burner.

"Careful you don't hurt yourself," Dad warns. "What's the occasion?"

"I'm doing a test run of Granny Washington's famous lemonade recipe for our Lemonade Day project," I answer. "I'm the operations manager, so that's my job on the team."

"Well, if it's half as good as what your grandma makes, you'll sell out." My father pulls one of my braids.

"Yeah! Daddy's home!" Cole bounds through the back door, and Mom follows.

"Dinner should be about ready." Mom kisses my father on the cheek. "I need to make a salad, and we'll be set."

She walks to the sink to wash her hands.

"Get back!" I shoo Cole away when he circles around the pitcher. I dump the heated sugar water in with the squeezed lemon and stir it up.

"Can't wait to try it." Mom looks over my shoulder as I work.

Happy to be the center of attention for once I work the spoon around the bottom of the pitcher slowly.

"A special drink calls for special dishes." Mom pulls out drinking glasses with flowers carved on them that she only uses when she has friends over.

"The lemonade needs to cool a few minutes, and then it'll be ready." I set the pitcher in the fridge.

"What a treat." Dad gives me a side hug. "Thanks, Sophie. It's been a while since I had Mom's special recipe."

I smile and show all my teeth, anxious for dinner to be ready. Wait until they try my lemonade!

CHAPTER 6

Master Plan

"This tastes like beach water." Cole puckers his lips as if he's been sucking something terrible.

Dad gulps from his glass, and then turns his lips down.

"Uh, Sophie, what exactly did you put in this lemonade?" asks Mom. She wipes her tongue with her paper napkin as if that will remove the taste.

"Just sugar, water, and lemon juice," I answer, taking a small sip.

It's terrible! I blink back tears.

"I don't know what went wrong, Mom! I just boiled the sugar and water and added lemon juice."

"Where'd you get the sugar?" Mom asks.

"The pantry. It was in a measuring cup with a plastic lid on it."

She starts laughing. "That explains it! You used salt. Remember? Cole knocked over the salt container this morning, and I poured what was left in a measuring cup."

My face feels hot. "Sorry, Dad. I wanted the lemonade to be like Granny Washington's."

"That's an honest mistake, sweetie," he answers. "You can try it again another time."

Cole puts his hand over his mouth to cover his giggles. I don't know why he's laughing about the lemonade. It's his fault it's messed up. If he wasn't so clumsy, Mom wouldn't have put salt in a container like that, and I wouldn't have gotten confused. Mom gets us all water bottles, and we finish dinner. I feel better after I fill up with the yummy King Ranch chicken and even a few bites of salad. I usually don't like vegetables, but Mom's mixed in a sweet dressing with the lettuce that makes even the radish pieces not taste so bad. She should be a contestant on one of those cooking shows.

"How'd things go in your second meeting with Mrs. Gentry?" Dad asks Mom.

"Super!" she answers. "I showed her the final business plan for her candle business. She has a unique product, and I think it'll sell well on the Internet. We're meeting with the bank next week to request a business loan. She's making a new lavender and honey candle that smells wonderful."

"You're still helping us on Thursday, right?" I hold my fork.

"Sure, sweetie," Mom nods her head. "We need to get things rolling, since it's coming up so soon."

I tell her about Carly's idea to donate money we earn to the animal shelter, and how Nathan's father will probably be our sponsor.

"Great! We'll write out a list of all the supplies we need at our meeting," says Mom. "We can also estimate how much money we think we'll make and decide how much we want to donate to the shelter. Letting customers know that a portion of the money they spend at your stand will be going to a good cause is a wonderful idea."

"I'll draw more pictures for our signs tonight!" pipes in Cole.

"I'm so proud of both of you kids." Mom holds her hands across her heart. "Learning about business and helping others!"

"Lemonade Day sounds like it will be quite the event," says Dad. "Where's it being held?"

"In the school parking lot," I answer. "Oh, and I forgot, Dad. As operations manager, I'm responsible for making the lemonade *and* the actual lemonade stand. Can you help with that?"

"I'd better check for instructions on building one on the Internet tonight," Dad chuckles. "You seem to be as good at ordering people around as your mom, Sophie."

"You wouldn't have it any other way," Mom lightly punches his arm.

"Your mother and I are going to take a walk." Dad pushes his chair back from the table after we finish eating.

At the word "walk," Bertram's ears perk up, and he starts whimpering.

"Kids, get the dishes rinsed and loaded in the dishwasher while we're gone." Mom grabs the dog's leash.

"Don't try to sneak off to the restroom." I warn Cole, as soon as my parents shut the door. Whenever there's work to be done, he's got to use it.

"I didn't drink a lot since all we had was water." He makes fun of my failed lemonade.

"If you weren't so clumsy and didn't drop the salt container, it wouldn't have gotten messed up." I wrap my arms around my chest.

"It's not my fault you put the wrong thing in your recipe."

"Whatever." I drop the argument. "Just come help, so we'll be done in here."

I hand him the broom and start working on the dishes. While I rinse off the salad plates, I brainstorm ideas to make our lemonade stand the best it can be. We should put posters advertising our stand all over town. We need to make as much money as we can. I can't wait to shop with Chloe at the mall. I forgot to tell Mom about Carly's suggestion to bring pets to adopt. We'd better make sure that animals are allowed at Lemonade Day.

"All done!" Cole shakes crumbs from the dustpan into the garbage, and then grabs his electronic tablet out of the wicker basket on the counter. My parents don't like him playing video games during the week, but I let him slide because I don't want to waste time arguing.

After I start the dishwasher, I sit down with a notebook to write down ideas to bring up at our next meeting. My chest gets tight as I look at all we have to do. Lemonade Day seems fun, but it also seems like a lot of work. I hope we can get it all together in less than two weeks.

CHAPTER 7

Team Work

Thursday after school, I float to the carpool line. I have plenty of Lemonade Day plans to share with my friends. After Dad and Mom got back from their walk the other night, he and I searched for information on how to build a lemonade stand on the Internet. We found a neat one we can make using four crates and wooden rods.

"We can spray paint it!" I pointed out some photos of light blue and yellow lemonade stands on the computer screen.

"I want to help too!" Cole piped up.

"Paint in the far corner of the backyard," said Mom. "That's going to be a big mess."

"We'll make sure to put everything back in its place." Dad kissed her on the mouth.

"Stop!" I blushed and covered my eyes.

"Eww! Yuck." For once, Cole agreed with me.

Now that the big meeting day is here, with Mom as our mentor, I want to jump up and down. There's a week and a half left to get things ready, and we have a lot to do.

"Over here, guys!" I wave Chloe, Nathan, and Carly over to where Cole and I are standing. Someone elbows me in the ribs, and I wince. Restless after being cooped in classrooms all day, my schoolmates act like they've been chugging energy drinks.

"Boys, get away from the curb!" a monitor warns some fifth graders, who are hopping too close to the street. The pickup area is crammed with people waiting for their rides.

"Wait 'til you taste my lemonade!" I twist around in my seat after we pile in Mom's SUV. Chloe and Carly are in the middle row with me, and Nathan sits in the back with Cole.

Yesterday afternoon, I made both regular and Berry Special lemonade. It's delicious, if I do say so myself. After Mom and I finished making it, I hid the pitchers in back of the fridge, so Dad and Cole wouldn't find them and drink them all up.

"It's a good thing Mom helped Sophie with her lemonade this time," says Cole. "Her first batch tasted like that stuff you gargle with when you have a sore throat."

Seeing me frown through the rear-view mirror, Mom interrupts. "That was an honest mistake, son. I sampled Sophie's new lemonade, and it's great."

"I love sweet lemonade!" Chloe waves her hands. "Have you drawn any more pictures to advertise our stand, Cole? Maybe we can choose some today and have photocopies made of them."

"I have two more sketches," Cole answers. "I'll show you when we get home." Excited to have Chloe's attention, he pulls out his joke book.

"Why was the lemon by himself? Because the banana split."

"What do you get when you cross a cat and a lemon? A sour puss."

"Those jokes are so cheesy, Dude!" Nathan hits the back of the seat and laughs.

"Tell me about it." I grimace like I'm in pain. "Cole has a bad joke for every occasion."

"You're just jealous 'cause you're not funny." He sticks out his tongue. In the front seat, Mom has her "cut it out," look, so I don't say anything else.

"Speaking of cats," says Carly. "I asked the director of the animal shelter about letting us bring pets to our lemonade stand. She thinks it's a great idea. The shelter is doing the paperwork to get it approved."

"We should probably limit it to no more than three or four animals," Mom suggests. "And we'll need to make sure they are in cages or are leashed. You'll be busy working the lemonade stand, and we don't want too much going on."

As we pull up to our driveway, Bertram barks and snarls from the backyard.

"What a pretty poochie!" Carly exclaims.

"Does it bite?" Nathan's eyes widen at Bertram when we step out of the car.

"He seems like a guard dog, but Bertram's as gentle as a teddy bear." I reassure him as we step toward the garage.

"Yeah, he wouldn't hurt a flea," says Cole, walking over to the fence to pet our dog.

"Come on, Carly," I steer her toward the garage before she gets distracted and joins him. "This way."

41

When I walk into the garage I see why Mom parked her SUV in the driveway. There're about ten medium-sized cardboard boxes filling the space.

"What's that?" I ask.

"Materials for Mrs. Gentry's candles," Mom answers. "She's picking them up later." She fishes her keys from the bottom of her purse, opens the lock, and steps inside the house.

I remember that I didn't clear off the shoe rack in the laundry room yesterday, so I have my friends leave their shoes at the doorway before we follow.

"Close the garage door when you come in," I yell over to Cole, who's scratching Bertram's nose through the fence.

"Your house is so pretty, Sophie." Carly admires a vase of yellow roses on the counter. One of Mrs. Gentry's candles sits beside it in a blue pottery container. Mom must have been burning it earlier because the house smells like lavender.

"Look at Cole!" Nathan laughs at a baby picture of him sucking his thumb and holding a baby blanket on an end table. We set our backpacks down by some chairs at the kitchen table and get ready to work.

"Here's some snacks, and then let's get started." Mom sets a platter with cookies, cheese, and crackers between us, and I bring out the lemonade.

"Sweet! Think I'll come home with you after school every day!" Nathan pours a glass of the Berry Special lemonade into a clear, plastic cup. The frozen berries I added yesterday have melted, so the drink looks pink. Mom put in cut slices of lemon to make it even fancier.

"Mmmm…this is delicious!" Nathan raves. "We should charge extra for this one."

"I agree," says Mom. "This drink includes more ingredients than regular lemonade, so it should be priced higher."

"Awesome!" Carly takes a sip. "Sophie's Berry Special lemonade is my new favorite drink!"

"The regular one is really good too." Chloe samples some. "My bestie is the best lemonade drink maker, ever!"

Once we're settled and snacking, Mom pulls out five pieces of paper. "Let's make lists of tasks we have to do for every area of our business," she says. "Once we're done, we'll combine this information to make up our business plan. We can turn those into the judges at the actual Lemonade Day event."

"We sure have a lot to do." My stomach tightens like I've done twenty sit-ups. "What if we don't get it all done in time?"

"It's not like you're being graded for this, sweetie." Mom pats my back. "The point is for you to learn about being an entrepreneur. Have fun with it."

Barking at the back door interrupts our conversation.

"Is Cole still out there?" asks Chloe.

"He stayed with your dog when we came in," says Carly.

"What in the world are you doing?" Mom opens the door to find Cole chasing Bertram around the garage.

"Get back here!" Cole cries, trying to grab hold of his fur. Something red flaps in our dog's mouth.

In his right hand, Cole holds one of Chloe's new shoes.

CHAPTER 8

The Maze

"I just bought those at the mall last weekend!" Chloe puts her hands at the side of her face.

The once-new shoe resembles a ripped-up dishrag.

"Cole! Stop Bertram!" I chase after them.

"Woof! Woof!" Bertram zig zags, and my brother and I follow. If I wasn't so worried about our dog destroying the garage, hopping through the cardboard maze might be fun.

Like the inside of our house, our garage is usually neat. Racks on the walls hold our bikes, and organized cans of paint and labeled bins with hardware materials line built-in shelves.

Bertram leaps over one of the smaller stacks of boxes, and it wobbles.

"Be careful!" Yells Mom, as I lunge to keep it from toppling. Too late.

There's a crash as at least fifteen blue pottery containers shatter on the cement floor like a fallen sky.

"Bad dog!" Mom grabs Bertram's collar and yanks the shoe from his mouth. "Mrs. Gentry's candle holders are ruined!"

Bertram tucks his tail and whimpers.

"Look at this mess!" Mom shakes her head, dangling the chewed-up shoe by her fingertips.

"I'm so sorry, Chloe!" I exclaim. She bites her lip.

One shoe's completely shredded, and the other has teeth marks in the fabric.

My head feels like a steaming tea kettle. I turn to Cole. "Why were you out here with Bertram anyway? You should've been helping us with our Lemonade Day project!"

"I wanted to play with him a little bit before I came in." Cole lowers his head. "He gets lonely while we're in school. When I opened the gate to go in the backyard, he almost knocked me over to get to the garage."

Bertram loves to eat shoes. Dad almost didn't let us keep him after he ruined an expensive pair of his loafers. We've put him in doggy obedience school, but he needs to go back.

"I told you kids to keep your shoes in the laundry room." says Mom.

"The shoe rack was full, so we left them out here." I look down at the ground.

"Didn't I ask you to get your old shoes and boots out of there?" Mom puts her hands on her hips. "You know you shouldn't leave shoes where Bertram can get them."

My face feels warm. I wish my mother wouldn't fuss at me in front of my friends.

"Sorry, Mom. I forgot."

"It's okay, Sophie." Chloe puts her hand on my shoulders. "I know you didn't mean it."

"Cole, take Bertram to the backyard." Mom points her hand. "We'll replace your shoes, Chloe. Come on kids, let's go inside. Sophie and Cole can clean this mess up later."

"Your dog sure is fast," says Nathan, as we leave the garage. "Wish I had my radar gun with me. I wonder what his velocity level was when he jumped over that box?"

"You would think of velocity at a time like this," I answer.

I feel like a popped balloon as I sit back down at the kitchen table. Mom and Mrs. Gentry have been working hard to get her candle business going. And I know that Chloe saved for those shoes for a long time. Seems as if I'm always messing up.

"We've got about an hour before your parents come for pickup, kids," says Mom. "Let's accomplish something."

Despite all the confusion in the garage, we get a lot done. First, we make a budget for supplies.

"We'll need seventy-five dollars from our sponsor to build our stand, get lemons, sugar, and berries for the lemonade, buy plastic cups and napkins, and print out fliers to advertise." Nathan figures after he looks up materials prices on the Internet.

We decide to charge a dollar for our regular lemonade and a dollar fifty cents for the Berry Special.

"I heard that over a thousand people visited Lemonade Day last year," says Mom. "Let's shoot to sell at least three hundred cups of lemonade."

"I'll type up a computer spreadsheet that'll show how much money we spend and how much we make," says Nathan. "If we sell three hundred cups of the Berry Special lemonade we could earn four hundred and fifty dollars."

While we're working on the budget, Cole draws a couple more posters that Carly will make copies of to hang up around the school and neighborhood.

"Great job, kids!" says Mom as we start clearing up. "We're off to a good start! I have some beverage dispensers in the attic we can use to pour the lemonade from and some other decorations, so we won't have to buy those."

"Can anybody come over to our house on Saturday, around eleven or noon?" I ask. "Dad's going to help me make our lemonade stand."

"Sure, I'll ask my mom," Chloe answers. "Sounds like fun!"

"Make sure to wear some old shoes," Nathan jokes. "Sorry I can't make it. I have to work on my science project."

"I'm volunteering at the animal shelter Saturday morning," says Carly. "But I'll come over after I'm finished."

I give Chloe a pair of my flip flops to wear home.

"Here's a check to replace your shoes." Mom hands her an envelope as she's heading out the door.

"Guess I'll have to go to the mall again this weekend," Chloe says with a smile. "Thanks so much, Mrs. Washington."

After my friends drive away with their parents, Cole and I sweep up the mess in the garage.

"Be careful not to cut yourselves around those pottery pieces," Mom warns.

"If she's so worried about us getting hurt, why doesn't she help us?" Cole mumbles.

"Be quiet before she comes up with something else for us to do," I whisper, grabbing the dust pan.

We work together to scoot the heavy boxes out of the way, making sure not to leave any pieces of sharp glass behind. Within a half-an-hour, the mess is cleared away.

"Nice work," Mom peeks through the garage door. "Alexis twisted her ankle in ballet class, so Mrs. Gentry isn't coming to pick these up until tomorrow."

She holds up a calculator and starts punching. "Ten of Mrs. Gentry's pottery containers were broken. They cost five dollars each, so you owe her fifty dollars. I looked up Chloe's shoes on the Internet, and they cost another fifty dollars, including sales tax."

"But it wasn't our fault, Mom!" I raise my palms. "Bertram did it! And if Cole had come inside the house like the rest of us, this wouldn't have happened."

"Both of you are responsible in my opinion." Mom wraps her arms across her chest. "Cole shouldn't have opened the gate, but you shouldn't have told your friends to leave their shoes in the garage, knowing how our dog behaves. Plus, you ignored my instructions to clear off the shoe rack, twice."

"I don't have a hundred dollars." I poke out my lip. "I only get five dollars a week for my allowance. How can I pay you back?"

"When life hands you lemons, make lemonade," says Mom. "You need to figure it out. I expect to have a plan about how you and Cole are going to work off or repay the money by tomorrow afternoon."

50

CHAPTER 9

Budget

After we come inside, Cole sits on the couch, flapping his arms like a chicken to make armpit farts. In the kitchen, Mom hums along to a song she listens to from her ear buds while she cooks.

"Do you have any money?" I stand in front of my brother.

"Why is money called dough?" He wiggles his eyebrows. "Because we all knead it."

"Cut it with the jokes, Cole." I stamp my foot. "This is serious. If we don't come up with a plan to repay Mom by tomorrow, she might not let us be in Lemonade Day, or worse."

"She'll do more to you, 'cause you're the oldest," he answers, and goes back to making gross noises.

"Seriously, Cole! Stop it!" I raise my hands. "I let you be on my Lemonade Day team, and this is how you repay me? And Mom's birthday is coming up. I want to get her a special bracelet I saw at the mall. If we can pay the money back, maybe we can still save to buy it."

He chews his lip for a second as he thinks. "I have ten dollars in my bank."

"Just ten dollars!" I wring my hands. "What happened to the check Granny Washington gave you when she came to visit last month?"

"I got a new super hero costume," he answers.

I snort. "You wasted twenty-five dollars on a Black Panther suit?!"

"It was fifteen dollars, and it was better than that bubble bath junk you bought!"

Seeing I'm getting nowhere with him, I clomp up to my room. On my dresser, my goldfish, Goldy, swims around a plastic plant in his bowl without a care in the world.

The most exciting thing in his day is when I drop him some fish flakes. I'd love to switch places with him right now.

I grab my piggy bank from beside the fish bowl and flop down with it on my pink bedspread. When I turn the porcelain bank upside down, the five dollars Mrs. Gentry gave me for watching Alexis, a dime, and an orange barrette fall out. It'll take me a million years to repay Mom.

We hope to earn three hundred dollars from our lemonade stand, with plans to return seventy-five dollars back to our sponsor. Another seventy dollars will be donated to the animal shelter. I get a piece of paper and my sparkly, purple pencil to figure out how much money each of us should expect from what's left.

"Three hundred minus seventy-five is two hundred twenty-five," I say out loud. "Two hundred twenty-five minus seventy-five is one hundred and fifty."

"Divide that by five people, and we get thirty dollars each." After I figure out the equation, I set my pencil on my night stand and shake my head.

Thirty measly dollars! With Cole's portion, that makes sixty dollars we can use to pay Mom back. Adding the fifteen dollars we have in our piggy banks, we'll have a total of seventy-five dollars to pay our debt, and still owe our mother twenty-five dollars.

My head throbs. Cole and I won't get to keep any of the money we earn from Lemonade Day, and Mom'll make us do extra chores to make up the balance. I won't have money to buy her a special bracelet for her birthday, either.

"This is so not fair!" I wrap my arms around my chest and frown.

At dinner, I don't say much. Dad's so tired from working that he doesn't notice it's quieter than usual.

"A kid fell off his bike and came in with a chipped tooth at closing time," he says once we sit down. "I had to put on a special filling. It's a good thing he was wearing his helmet, or the damage would have been worse."

"Safety is so important." Mom spoons him an extra scoop of mashed potatoes. "Always wear your helmets when you ride your bikes and when you skate outside, kids."

She had mercy on us and went light on the vegetables today. Some nights we have salad, along with another vegetable, but today it's just green beans, my favorite. I eat an extra helping with my meatloaf.

"There's my healthy eater." Dad gives me a thumbs up. "I forgot to ask…how'd the Lemonade Day meeting go?"

"Good," I answer. "We planned almost everything. Can we build the lemonade stand this weekend? I invited the team over to help."

"That should be fine," Dad stands up and puts his empty plate in the sink. "You kids can come with me to the hardware store to pick out supplies."

"Speaking of supplies, we had a little mishap in the garage today," says Mom, and I wring my napkin.

"Sophie and Cole broke some of Mrs. Gentry's candle holders and will be paying for the replacement costs with their Lemonade Day earnings."

"It's going to take all the money we make, Mom!" I chew my bottom lip. "We have to pay back the sponsor for supplies, and we're donating money to the animal shelter too."

"You're in luck, because I found some crates and pieces of wood up in the attic," she answers. "That should reduce your supply bill and the amount of money you'll need from your sponsor, so you'll have something left over."

"Thanks, Mom! That's great!" The cloud that's surrounded me all evening lifts as I get a new idea. I call Chloe for her opinion.

CHAPTER 10

The Mother of Invention

"Good thinking!" Chloe cheers over the phone. "We can use things we already have to make our lemonade stand! We've got hundreds of extra paper napkins, plastic cups, and straws at my house from our family reunion last summer. Mom changed her party theme, so we never used them."

"What color are they?" I ask.

"The napkins and straws are yellow." says Chloe. "And the cups are clear."

"Perfect!" I say with a smile. "Look for other things to decorate our booth with around your house. We can have it looking great for next-to-nothing. We'll have to buy lemons, berries, and sugar for the drinks though."

While I'm on the phone, Mom pulls out the crates and drink dispensers, and Cole helps her take them out to the garage. Dad finds some leftover cans of spray paint in a laundry room cabinet.

I finish my call with Chloe and start a group text with the other kids.

Let's sell snacks. Suggests Nathan. **My Dad said we can borrow his Fun Plex popcorn machine.**

Awesome! Says Carly. **I can also make chocolate chip and sugar cookies.**

After we click off the phone, I stand and do a cheerleader jump.

"That must have been some phone call!" Mom sets down the dish towel she's folding and laughs.

"To earn more money, we're selling food, along with the drinks at our lemonade stand," I tell her. "We can probably double our profits! And using things we already have makes us only have to get forty dollars from our sponsor."

"Great! Necessity is the mother of invention," Mom says.

"What's that mean?" I ask.

"It's an old saying that means that when we want something, our minds search for ways to make it happen," she explains. "Since you need money to pay back your debt, you're getting creative to find ways to increase your income. With snacks, your lemonade booth should attract even more customers. You're learning all the steps to becoming a top entrepreneur."

>>>>>>>>>><<<<<<<<<<

Saturday can't come quick enough.

As soon as I wake up, I throw on jeans and a tee shirt, make my bed, brush my teeth, and wash my face.

"It's time to make our lemonade stand!" I tell Goldy as I drop some fish food flakes in his bowl. As if to answer, he puckers his lips and swishes his feathery tail.

When I bounce downstairs the rest of the family is already in the kitchen. Mom's at the stove making bacon, turkey sausage, and eggs, while my father mixes batter to use on his new, waffle iron. The coffee maker drip, drip, drips, filling the room with a nutty caramel, scent.

"What time are we gonna build the lemonade stand?" asks Cole, grabbing a piece of bacon off a plate on the counter.

"I guess after we eat," says Dad.

"Chloe and Carly are coming over to help," I say. "Chloe's stopping by the mall first to get her new shoes."

"Tell her not to wear them over here because I don't want to pay more money, if Bertram eats them," Cole teases and pulls another slice of bacon off the plate.

"Get away from the stove and go to the table, Cole," Mom fusses. "You're going to finish all the food before we can sit down."

Across the kitchen, Bertram sits by his water bowl. He watches Cole nibble on the bacon with round eyes, until my brother slips him a piece. Bertram tries to be quiet, so he can get more goodies, but Mom has an eagle eye.

"Can you take the dog out, son? I don't want him in here begging while we're trying to eat." Cole grabs him by the collar and slips into the garage.

"I can't wait to put our lemonade stand together!" I walk over to watch Dad pour batter on the waffle iron.

"I'm looking forward to it myself," he says. "I saw some neat examples on the Internet last night. This is a fun project that you can use to raise money at other times too."

"Yeah, we could sell lemonade right here in our neighborhood when it's hot outside." Cole returns from the back door. "And become bazillionaires!"

"Does a bazillionaire exist?" Mom scrambles some eggs in the skillet and laughs.

"With the way inflation's going, we may have some by the time the kids are grown," answers Dad, cutting up some strawberries to eat with our waffles.

The delicious breakfast smells make me feel like sticking my tongue out like Bertram. When the food is finally done, I rush to the table.

"This looks sooo good!" I pour maple syrup on my waffle, add some berries, and take a huge bite. "Next time, let's get some whipped cream like they have at restaurants."

"Good idea, Sis!" Cole says, smacking his lips.

"You already have enough sugar with all that syrup you poured on your waffles." Mom shakes her head. "You guys will be bouncing off the walls by the time the girls get here."

My BFF must have gone to the mall at opening time, because she rings our door bell at ten thirty.

"Ready to work on our stand?" Chloe asks, when I open the door. Even though it's Saturday, she looks put together in a blue tee shirt with a glittery design on the front and a hair bow.

"See you later, Mrs. Hopkins!" I wave to her mother as she backs out of the driveway.

"Come see what Mom got for us to use!" I pull Chloe inside by the arm.

"Your shirt sleeve is ripped," I say, surprised, since she's always so particular. I notice she's also wearing older tennis shoes.

"My mother said I shouldn't wear my good clothes since we're building things," she explains.

"The spray paint we're using isn't washable," says Dad as we step into the kitchen, "so that might be a good idea."

"It's building time!" Cole jumps up from his seat and shakes his behind. "Our lemonade stand is gonna kick butt!"

"Watch your language, son!" Mom moves from the kitchen sink. "I'll finish up with the breakfast dishes. You all go on outside. Let me get you kids some of your father's old tee shirts to toss on over your clothes before you paint."

"Wait a minute! You're just using this as an excuse to get rid of my old shirts that're boxed up in the closet!" says Dad.

Mom turns and winks, and he laughs.

"While she's getting your smocks, let's move the materials to the backyard," Dad suggests.

We step through the back door out into the garage. The crates and wood that my parents and Cole had neatly stacked for our lemonade stand are in a jumbled pile, and one of the long pieces of wood is broken in half.

"Woof! Woof!" Bertram barks from the corner of the room, and my heart sinks.

CHAPTER 11

Lemonade Stand

"What's Bertram doing in here?" I shriek.

"Mom told me to let him out before we got breakfast." Cole cowers, and the dog tucks his tail.

"She meant for you to put him in the back yard! Not in here with all our Lemonade Day stuff!"

Exasperated, I link my hands behind my head. Bertram must have been chasing his tail in circles in this place. Thank goodness, Mrs. Gentry picked up her candle containers yesterday.

I crouch to get a closer look and breathe out. None of the glass drinking dispensers Mom put out for our lemonade are broken.

"It's okay, Sophie." Dad rubs my back. "This wooden pole I was going to use to hold up the banner is broken, but I have some more like it in the attic. Come with me, Cole, let's get another one."

I glare at my brother as he follows Dad. I wish my parents had let me do this project with just my friends. I ball my hands into fists for a minute as I calm down.

"Mmm...mmm...mmm.." Bertram whines.

Chloe walks over to our trembling dog and scratches him behind the ears. "Poor Poochie, everybody's been on your case this week."

I set a knocked over crate upright. "You oughta be the main one mad at him, Chloe, since he destroyed your favorite shoes."

"I got a cuter pair at the mall this morning." Chloe perks up. "They're lavender, with yellow flowers sewn on. It would've taken me months to save up for them."

Bertram approaches me with a droopy tail and rubs his head on my leg. My heart melts as I look into his wide eyes.

"All right. I guess it's Bertram to the rescue then!" I hug him to accept his apology.

"Ruff!" He licks me on the cheek.

"You should give Cole a break too, Sophie," says Chloe. "He *is* only eight-years-old. Remember when we were his age and tried to help your mom cook dinner faster by turning the oven from 300 degrees to 500? Smoke filled the kitchen, and the lasagna was burnt black!" She shook her head. "Your mom didn't even get mad at us. She knew we were trying to help. It's not like your brother's been pranking you or anything."

"I guess I have been hard on him," I nod. "I just want our lemonade stand to be great."

"It will be," says Chloe. "Relax."

Dad comes back in, and Cole lags behind, like he's about to take medicine.

"Sorry for yelling at you, Cole." I step to him before he can speak. "I know you're only trying to help."

"You mean you're not mad at me anymore?" He scoots back in disbelief.

"No, I'm over it," I answer. "I shouldn't have been so hard on you."

Cole pumps his fist in the air. "Yes! I'm gonna be the best team member ever! You'll see!"

"That's what I'm talking about!" Dad wraps his arms around us both. "Brothers and sisters working together! Now, let's assemble this lemonade stand!"

"Should we wait for Carly?" Chloe asks.

"She said she might be a little late, since she's volunteering at the animal shelter," I answer. "Let's start."

Each of us grabs something to take out to the patio.

"First, we get the crates together," says Dad. He stacks three crates, side-by-side, and then puts the other three on top of them. The crates face in alternate opposite directions.

"Why aren't they going the same way?" asks Cole.

"You can use some for shelves to store things," my father explains. He hands each of us a hammer and some nails and points to the areas we need to put them in. "Connect the pieces together. Watch that you don't hit your hands."

"I'll help you, Cole." I hold the crate steady while he hammers.

Not too hot, not too cool, clear, and sunny, it's the perfect day to work on our lemonade stand. I hope the weather is as nice on the actual Lemonade Day.

"My little carpenters are at work!" Mom comes out holding three of old Dad's tee shirts and a yellow sheet.

"Put these on when you're ready to start painting. And please remember to move out into the yard with that spray paint can. I don't want paint on my patio furniture."

She watches us work for a few minutes and then clasps her hands. "While you're putting the stand together, I'll bring out craft supplies we can use to decorate."

"Ooooh...can I help with that?" Chloe stops hammering. "I love decorating."

"Everyone can help, once we get this part done," says Dad.

After we connect the crates, he adds a few more nails to make the stand extra sturdy. Then he drills in wooden poles on each side of the stand.

"We'll add a sign to these later," he explains. "Now it's time to paint. Here, grab hold of each end of the stand, and let's move it to the other side of the yard. Hold on, kids, I need to get the spray paint out from the garage."

"Cole! Come help!" I yell as my brother runs to the patio when Dad walks away.

Thinking we want to play, Bertram bounds after him.

"Not now! I'll throw the ball with you later." Cole returns and scratches the dog's head with one hand and holds his other hand behind his back.

I pull one of Dad's old tee shirts over my head, hand one to Chloe, and toss one at Cole's feet.

"Quit goofing around." I frown at him.

"Let's get this party started!" Cole pulls a can from behind his back.

"What're you doing!" I yell. "Don't get paint on us!"

He pries off the red lid, aims the can our way, and presses the button.

"OMG!" Chloe jumps, as a white toothpaste-like stream squirts out and sticks to the front of her shirt.

"Don't get that on my hair!" I hold my hands over my two braids.

"Woof! Woof!" Bertram shakes his fur to escape from the goo.

"Put that silly string down, and let's get back to work!" Dad booms behind us. "It's time to paint."

"I'm ready!" Cole stops his prank as Dad holds up the spray paint.

"Shake it up first." My father rolls the can between his hands a few seconds to mix the liquid and then presses the spray button.

"Yippee!" Cole pumps his fist in the air as the brown crates turn white. "My turn! My turn!"

"The things you kids get excited about!" Dad hands him the can and laughs.

Chloe and I stand back as Cole spray paints, so we don't end up looking like snowmen.

We each take a turn spraying the crates to make sure it's fully colored with paint.

"I love it!" Chloe stands back from the stand when we're finished. It's bright white, and we didn't get a lot of paint on ourselves or the grass.

"Good job!" I give my brother a fist bump before he runs to the patio.

"I looked up a neat idea for making an awning to block the sun." Mom walks over while we admire our work. "Want to try it while the paint on the stand dries?"

"Sure," says Chloe. "What do we do?"

"The clean half of this sheet can be the awning." Mom cuts the yellow fabric in half with some scissors. "I'll hold this ruler down, and you spray paint on lines."

"Cool!" I exclaim as Chloe sprays alternating white lines on the material. It reminds me of a yellow candy cane. The ruler acts like a stencil to keep the lines straight.

"It's getting hot out here," says Mom. "Anybody want a drink?" She goes inside and brings out some water bottles and chips, and we snack while waiting to put finishing touches on our lemonade stand.

After everything dries, Mom attaches the awning to the wooden poles with an old curtain rod. I can't stop smiling.

"I've got to send a picture of this to Nathan and Carly!" Chloe pulls out her cell phone. "Stand over there, Sophie."

I feel Cole moving behind my back as I grin next to our Lemonade Day stand, turn and see him giving me rabbit ears.

"Get out of the way, boy." I shoo him over toward where Mom and Dad sit on the patio, and get ready to pose for another picture.

"Wait a minute, Carly just sent a text message." Chloe looks down at her phone. "She has an emergency."

CHAPTER 12

On the Loose

"Emergency?" I feel goosebumps on my arm. "What's going on? Is she okay?"

Chloe dials Carly's cell phone and puts her on speaker as soon as she answers. "Hey, girl. Just got your message. Is everything alright?"

"I'm so sorry I didn't make it to put the lemonade stand together!" Carly sounds nervous. "I'm at the shelter by myself. Ms. Vincent, the coordinator, went to the store for some extra dog food, and I forgot to lock the dog cages after I gave them water. The dogs got out, and I'm trying to gather them up. I called my parents to help, but they aren't picking up their phones."

Ruff! Ruff! I hear barking in the background. Bertram freezes and perks his ears up.

"That's terrible, Carly!" exclaims Chloe. "How many dogs are loose?"

"Fifteen, twenty...I'm not sure! I've got to get them back inside before they get hurt or lost. And if Ms. Vincent sees how irresponsible I've been, she might fire me from my volunteer job! Sparky! Come back here!"

There's a dial tone as the call drops.

"That's awful!" I say. "Poor Carly."

"I hope nothing happens to those dogs," says Chloe. "A stray got hit by a car in my neighborhood a couple of weeks ago."

I race over to the patio, where my parents are relaxing on our outdoor, patio sofa. Beside them, Cole bounces on his pogo stick.

"Dad! Can you take us to the animal shelter?" I wave my hands around wildly. "Carly needs our help!"

"What in the world?" Mom sets her glass down on our wooden, picnic table and raises her eyebrow.

"Please Mom, she needs us!" I hold my hands like I'm praying. "The dogs have gotten out!"

"Your friend's at the animal shelter by herself?" Dad stands.

"The director left her there alone while she went to get some more pet food," Chloe explains. "She still hasn't gotten back yet, and Carly's freaking out. Carly's parents aren't answering her calls, and the phone went dead while we were talking to her."

"That shelter is just a few blocks away," says Mom. "It wouldn't hurt to check it out. Cole and I'll stay here. All that fur would make my allergies go crazy."

"Okay, let me get my keys," Dad stretches his legs.

When he makes it to the garage a few minutes later, Chloe and I are already strapped in our seat belts.

"There's definitely never a dull moment with you kids." He chuckles as he starts the ignition.

I sit on the edge of my seat the entire five-minute, drive. "Try to call Carly again, Chloe!" I turn toward my friend.

"Her phone's still dead." She shakes her head after punching the number again.

Sitting at the end of a quiet, tree-lined, street, the one-story, animal shelter building is sky blue and has black images of dogs and cats painted on it. The empty parking lot looks like a doggy park. Ten dogs of different breeds jump and play on the cracked asphalt like old friends. A German shepherd races across the pavement, and Carly follows, blonde hair streaming.

"There she is!" I point my finger.

"Here, Sparky!" Carly calls.

"Let's get out to help her!" I reach to open the passenger door.

"Wait a minute, sweetie," says Dad. "Let me think about the best way to do this." He sits still a second, and then steps out of the SUV and opens the trunk.

"See if this gets their attention." He pulls out a bag of dog biscuits that Bertram loves and hands each of us a couple. "Hold the treat and move toward the entrance."

Dad whistles, and a beagle and a cocker spaniel mix stop running. Like Hansel and Gretel, they follow the trail of biscuits he drops to the animal shelter door.

"Here, doggie," I wave a biscuit, and two other dogs move in my direction.

"Awesome!" Carly grins, spotting us. Grabbing Sparky by the collar, she meets us at the door.

"This treat is yummy. Want a taste?" Chloe crouches beside a tiny chihuahua. It sniffs and tilts its head to the side, before taking a hesitant step toward her.

"Here's another one!" Dad leads a gray, furry dog to the door. "Hey, what are you doing?" Dad says with a laugh as the dog nuzzles his leg.

"Fuzzy likes you, Mr. Washington," Carly grins.

Within ten minutes, we have all the dogs back inside the shelter. Their individual cages line the wall like jail cells. Inside each cage, is a pet bed that looks like a mini trampoline and a water bowl. A few have rubber balls. I wrinkle my nose at the scent of wet fur and dog food.

"Whew! That was something else!" Carly smooths her hair, which is sticking up with static electricity. "My phone went dead, and I still haven't heard back from Ms. Vincent."

"Doesn't anybody else work here?" asks Dad.

"Usually," Carly answers. "But a couple of the other volunteers are sick, and another lady who works at the front desk is on vacation. Since I've been working here a while, Ms. Vincent thought I could handle things while she was gone." She holds her head. "The phone rang, and I forgot to lock the cages when I went to answer it. I let her, and the animals, down."

"Now, I wouldn't say that," Dad touches her shoulder. "The dogs are safe and sound. You had the good sense to call when you saw you were in over your head. Even some adults don't do that. You should be proud that Ms. Vincent thinks highly enough of you to trust you with such a responsibility."

"Thank you, Mr. Washington." Carly's face turns pink. "I really love working here, and I try to do my best."

In their cages, some dogs nap, others nudge balls with their noses, and many whimper with their paws hanging out of the metal bars.

"Poor things!" says Chloe. "They were having so much fun outside. I wish they could get out of here."

"They're sweet dogs!" says Carly. "I hope some of them get adopted on Lemonade Day. I already have a dog, a cat, a parrot, a snake, and a gecko, and my parents won't let me bring another pet home."

The gray dog named Fuzzy my father brought in scrapes his paws on the cage wires and howls. I walk over, and he pants and sticks out his tongue in a grin. The fluffy fur on its face looks like cotton balls.

"This one is sooo cute!" I turn to Dad.

"Don't even think about it." He shakes his head. "Bertram is a handful. Your mom would have a fit if we mentioned getting another dog."

"Too bad. So many of our pets need good homes." A tall lady with reddish brown hair falling out of a bun, sets some bags on a rolling cart near the entrance.

"Ms. Vincent!" Carly exclaims.

CHAPTER 13

The Tour

"Looks like you've kept things under control while I was gone, and even brought in some new potential patrons." The lady holds out her hand to Dad.

In her faded jeans and over-sized tee shirt with a "Save the animals," logo on it, she doesn't look like she's into fashion, but Ms. Vincent stands up straight like a ballet dancer. As soon as they see her, the animals stop whimpering and scratching at their cages.

"Welcome to the Woodbridge Animal Shelter. I'm Cynthia Vincent, director."

"This is my friend's dad, Mr. Washington," says Carly, "And this is Sophie and Chloe. They're on my Lemonade Day team."

"Pleased to meet you," Dad says with a smile. "This is quite a facility you have here. But we didn't actually come to adopt any animals today."

"They came to help me." Carly wrings her hands. "I left the cage doors open when the phone rang, and some of the dogs got out."

"With all these people not showing up today, I forgot to warn you about that." Mrs. Vincent hits her palm on her forehead. "The same thing happened to me a couple of days ago. The clasps on these cages are broken, and if they aren't shut a certain way, the dogs get out. I've got to call maintenance about that this week. There is so much that needs to be done around here."

"You mean you aren't mad at me?" Carly breathes a sigh of relief.

"I don't know what we'd do without you around here!" Ms. Vincent pats her shoulder. "Especially today, with all the other volunteers out. You've been such a great help!"

"We're excited to have the animal shelter as our Lemonade Day charity!" Chloe clasps her hands. "All the animals are adorable!"

"Yeah," I say. "I hope that we'll be able to get some adopted on Lemonade Day."

"We sure do appreciate your help for the cause," says Ms. Vincent. "Our goal is to have all these animals placed in good homes. Want to take a tour of the shelter?"

"Can we?" I turn to Dad.

"It'd be good for you girls to see who you'll be helping," he says, as he nods his head.

As we walk down the aisle, the dogs move forward. Their barking makes background music to our conversation.

"Some of these dogs are already set to be adopted," Ms. Vincent points at sheets of purple pages attached to their cages.

"Pepper here will be leaving in two weeks." She tosses a dog treat to a black and white terrier. "She's five years old and very active. We have fun playing fetch in the mornings. I'm sure going to miss her when she leaves."

We head to a kennel numbered twenty-six. A sign that says, "Hi, My Name is Maxine," is taped to the top.

"Maxine, you're still waiting!" Ms. Vincent points out the brown, black, and white bulldog mix. "She's a beautiful dog. We hope her owners find her soon."

Licking its lips, the dog begs for a treat.

"Why're you still here?" The director coos in a baby voice. "You're so cute!"

Maxine starts wagging.

"Look at that rear end," says Ms. Vincent. "You've got the happy tail. Yes, you do!"

We meet some of the other dogs, and the director hands us treats to feed them.

"Every day, Ms. Vincent records videos of the dogs, in case their owners are looking for them," says Carly. "The shelter does a great job of returning the pets to their owners or finding them new homes."

As we pass Fuzzy's cage, it starts chasing its tail.

"This beauty has been with us just three days," says Ms. Vincent. "She doesn't have a chip or a collar. Hopefully, the owners will come in soon."

"What happens if you can't find a home for the dogs?" Chloe looks into Fuzzy's round, black eyes.

"We're able to keep animals for weeks, or even months at this location, but sadly, if we get overcrowded, sometimes the animals have to be put to sleep," says Ms. Vincent. "I try to host adoption events at least twice a month to find good homes for all the animals."

"Arf! Arf!" A teeny bark sounds from the cage next door.

"It's the little one I brought in!" Chloe squats low to greet the chihuahua.

"Lady's been with us for a month and a half," says Ms. Vincent. "Her family left her here when they moved out of town."

Lady gives Chloe's finger a dainty lick.

"She looks like the perfect dog for you," I say.

"I see why you like working here," I turn to Carly.

"I want to help find homes for all these puppies," she says.

"Where are the cats?" asks Chloe, giving Lady one last glance as we move along.

"Their cages are on the other side of the building," Carly answers. "I don't work as much in that end, but there are plenty of sweet kitties over there."

"Maybe you ladies can come back and get a tour of that section another time," says Ms. Vincent. "I need to get the food bowls prepped now for the dogs' dinner."

"I can stay and help," says Carly. "While we were walking, I charged my phone and then texted my mom that the other volunteers didn't come in today, so she's picking me up at five thirty. My parents missed my call earlier because they were outside doing yard work. I'm happy they got that done before I got home!"

"It's almost four o'clock." Dad glances at his watch. "I didn't realize we'd been here for over an hour. It's about time for us to head home, girls. Chloe's parents are probably on their way to pick her up."

"Nice meeting you, Ms. Vincent," I wave as we head toward the exit. "Thanks for showing us around the shelter."

"And thank you guys for coming to help me out!" says Carly. "I don't know what I'd have done if you didn't show up."

"See you, sweetie!" Chloe waves at Lady when we pass by her kennel.

"Arf! Arf! Arf!" The dog barks in reply.

CHAPTER 14

Kickball

"I wish I'd been at the shelter with you guys," says Nathan. "It would've been fun chasing all those dogs around. I could have brought my radar gun to clock their speed for my experiment."

"You're such a science geek." I laugh at his comment.

"It was sad to see so many dogs needing a home," says Chloe. "Makes me want to raise even more money on Lemonade Day to help them."

"Now you see why I want to adopt all the animals," says Carly.

It's Monday, and we're meeting out on the playground after school again to go over last-minute details for Lemonade Day. The event is this weekend, and we still have a few things to get done.

Cole has art club, so I'll fill him in on our conversation on the ride home. Like normal, the playground is packed with kids waiting for their parents to pick them up. Some sixth-graders play kickball on the artificial grass. Our classmate, Toby, smiles our way when his team moves to home plate.

"Will you pay attention?!" I grumble to Chloe, as she peeks over at him. Toby shows his dimples back. The two of them won't admit they like each other, but the rest of the grade calls them ToChlo behind their backs.

I had a crush on Toby too, when he transferred to our school from Cleveland earlier this year. I'm not jealous that he's got a thing for my best friend, but I still get butterflies sometimes when he's around.

"Boo-yah!" Toby yells as he kicks a rubber ball toward the back wall.

"Show off!" Nathan frowns, when Toby raises his arms in the air, getting ready to run. Suddenly, a little boy runs onto the courtyard. He catches the ball in mid-air.

"It's Cole!" I put my hand over my mouth, laughing.

"Wait a minute!" Toby stomps his foot. "Hey, Sophie! Get your brother out of our game!"

"Sorry, Toby, but you need to kick the ball better!" I shout back.

"That's hilarious!" Nathan holds his stomach, cracking up.

"Interference! Let's do that play over." Toby frowns over at our table and then regroups with his team.

Avoiding the irritated kick ball team, Cole zig zags through the crowd to reach us. When he passes the monkey bars, he stares for a second, like he might swing across them if we hadn't already seen him.

"Great catch, Cole!" I high-five my brother once he reaches us.

"Way to show Toby who's boss," adds Nathan.

"You don't like Toby much, do you?" asks Carly.

"He thinks he's 'Mr.-All-That,'" Nathan answers.

Chloe nudges me with her elbow and winks. I shake my head.

"Art club ended early. Here's the fliers, guys." Cole sets a folder on the table.

"Cool!" says Carly, pulling them out. "You're so talented, Cole."

I've got to give my little brother credit. The drawings are great. The first one is the picture of me behind a lemonade stand, with a dog beside it. And the second has a dancing lemonade pitcher that has arms and feet. He's also made a third flier that says "Save the Animals: Support Lemonade Day," with the date, time and place in bubble letters.

"I came up with a list of everything we have left to do this week," Nathan pulls out a computer printout. "What do you think of this?" He shows us a piece of paper:

Lemonade Day To-Do List:

- Buy ingredients for cookies, popcorn, and lemonade.
- Make copies of fliers and post them.
- Decorate lemonade stand.
- Get change.
- Make lemonade.
- Get approval for pets to be at our stand from the school.

"That sounds about right," I scan it. "Nearly everything is done. The school is advertising Lemonade Day on its website and with a notice on the outside billboard. But we should ask other people we know to come out and buy from us."

"Before I go home, I'll make copies of the fliers in the front office," says Carly. "We can start hanging them up around the school and other places tomorrow."

"I'll put some fliers up at Fun Plex too," says Nathan.

"We should have done that this past weekend," I snap my finger. "More people would have seen it."

"A mother's group meets with smaller kids at Fun Plex on Wednesdays," Nathan answers.

"We can put a big sign where they hang out."

"Nathan, look out!" cries Carly. The rubber kickball bounces off the top of his head, and his glasses slide down his nose.

"OMG." Chloe giggles with her hands over her mouth.

"My bad. That was a foul," Toby holds his hands up like he's sorry but is smirking.

"He did that on purpose." Nathan balls his hands into a fists, his face red.

"I guess we messed with them first," I answer. "You okay?"

"Yeah," he answers, rubbing the back of his head.

"Sorry I caught that kick ball, guys," says Cole. "I couldn't help myself."

"Next time, stay out of other people's games, little bro," I advise.

"I should go make copies of these fliers before the front office closes," Carly grabs the drawings and stands up.

"Don't forget to ask about us bringing in pets while you're in there," reminds Chloe. "I hope we can find Fuzzy and some of the other dogs a home."

"Okay, meeting adjourned." I pick up my backpack.

"See you guys tomorrow." Chloe gets to her feet. "When I go home, I'll gather up some more things to decorate our lemonade stand. I have a super-cute mini-chalkboard we can write the prices of our drinks and snacks on."

We walk right past Toby and his friends on our way out. Giggling, Chloe waves.

"Good catch, Dude. Respect." Toby fist bumps Cole.

"You better work on that kick, Toby," I tease.

"I'll do that," he laughs.

"Hey, Smartypants, hope I didn't rattle your brain!" Toby turns to Nathan.

"Whatever," Nathan frowns.

CHAPTER 15

Principal's Office

"Cole and I can go to the office with you," I tell Carly, as the five of us walk back inside the school from the playground. "Mom just texted that she's running a few minutes late."

"Thanks," Carly answers. "I was nervous about asking Mrs. Jenkins if we can bring animals from the shelter to Lemonade Day myself."

"I'll come too," adds Nathan. "The more the merrier."

"If nobody adopts Lady, I wish I could take her," says Chloe. "I saw the *cutest* doggy sweater at the mall that I'd love to dress her in! Make sure you bring her to Lemonade Day, Carly, if we're able to have animals at our booth. I want to show her to my parents."

"If you end up with that dog it'll probably have its nails painted and go to the doggy spa," teases Nathan.

"You know it!" Chloe says and does a fashion model pose.

Without the usual crowd of kids gathering around lockers, our voices echo as we move down the hallway. To my left, Cole slides his sneakers on the tile, making an irritating squeak.

"Will you stop doing that?!" I complain.

"Sor-ry," he answers.

When we make it to the front of the school, Chloe turns to go out to the carpool line.

"See ya!" She hoists her backpack higher before she steps outside.

Nathan hits his hand on his forehead. "I forgot my radar gun in the science lab. I'm going to take some velocity readings of the speed of bowling balls at Fun Plex tonight. Better go get it."

"He really is like an absent-minded professor." Carly says, after he rushes off.

"I know, right?" I answer with a laugh.

At the principal's office, there's a floor-length glass window. You can see everything inside before you enter. Mrs. Jenkins, the school secretary, sits at the light-brown, wooden desk that's as long as a school bus. Behind her on the wall, is a banner with a fancy, giant letter "X" that represents Xavier Academy. Blocked from view by a metal beam stand two boys.

"What if they won't let us bring the animals?" Carly wrings her hands. "I'm scared to ask. I want the dogs to get good homes so badly."

"Seeing those cute, furry, faces in-person would probably make more people want to adopt them," I admit. "But if the school says no to the animals being there, we can still pass out pictures of them. And no matter what happens, we're giving the shelter money. That should definitely be a help."

"Can we bring Bertram to Lemonade Day too?" asks Cole. "He'll be lonely at home by himself."

"He's home alone any other time," I answer. "Why would this Saturday be any different?"

"He might smell other dogs on us when we get back and feel bad," Cole replies.

"It doesn't make any difference to me." I shrug my shoulders. "Ask Mom and Dad when we get home."

I turn the metal knob on the front office door, push it open and hold it for my brother and Carly to step in.

At the end of the counter, I notice a boy that we didn't see when we were outside. I get a fluttery feeling again when I recognize that it's Toby.

"Hey, champ!" Finished talking to Ms. Jenkins, Toby turns around and flashes his dimples at me and Cole. I smooth my hands over my braids.

"That was some catch you made earlier." He grins down at my little brother. "I'm going to practice my kicking, so you don't get me next time."

"Thanks, man!" Cole grins like he just got an autograph from his favorite NBA player.

"What're you guys doing in the principal's office?" Toby asks. "I know Xavier's spelling bee queen isn't in trouble."

"No, we're here to ask about having pets at our Lemonade Day stand." I look over at Mrs. Jenkins, who's just answered the phone. "The shelter is allowing us to bring them, but we need to get approval from the school to have animals at the event."

"That's that thing you invited me to do isn't it?" asks Toby. "Too bad we have our playoff game then. That would've been fun."

"It would have." I answer. "We had a hard time getting five people. Chloe and I came up with the idea to do Lemonade Day, and my parents had us add Cole. I was sad when you couldn't be on our team. We were lucky to get Carly to join."

Toby glances over my shoulder and smiles. "I'll bet it was slim pickings for team members after that."

"Yeah, we were happy to get anyone," I answer.

Eyes wide, Carly clears their throat and points behind me, and I turn around.

"Hi, Nathan."

CHAPTER 16

Busted

"I came back through to see if you guys were still here." Nathan's face is red.

"We're waiting for Mrs. Jenkins to finish up," I say. My hands feel clammy and my heart is beating fast. *Did he hear what I just said?* I stare at a red, white and blue banner on the wall that reads, "Xavier Rockets: Reach for the Stars."

"Welp, I need to head to practice." Toby pats Cole's afro before moving to the door. "See you later."

"Aye, Brainiac, what up?" He nods to Nathan, standing near the glass entrance.

While we wait to speak to the receptionist, Cole makes up jokes.

"What do you give a sick lemon?" He asks Nathan. "Lemonade. Get it, Lemon-aid."

"Man, you're too much!" Nathan shakes his head.

"You know it was funny!" Cole slaps him on the back.

I look over at Nathan while we wait. He avoids eye contact.

"I wonder which dogs we should bring if they allow it?" says Carly. "Fuzzy loves to be outside."

"Uh huh," I answer, nervously tapping my foot. I peek at Nathan out of the corner of my eye, but he ignores me.

After what feels like forever, Mrs. Jenkins finally gets off the phone. She peers at us over the counter.

"How may I help you?"

"Umm...we have a question about Lemonade Day." Carly rocks on her heels.

"Sign-ups for that ended a couple of weeks ago," Mrs. Jenkins interrupts. "The event is in two days. The school has me in charge of everything, and it's been quite the undertaking."

Frozen like a squirrel in front of a moving bike, Carly doesn't speak.

I step forward. "We already have a team signed up, remember? We're here to ask if we can include a part of our charity at our booth."

"What do you mean by that?" Mrs. Jenkins puts her hand on the counter.

"We want to bring dogs!" blurts Cole.

"Dogs? Well...that's highly unusual." The secretary raises her eyebrow.

"Our charity is the Woodbridge Animal Shelter." Carly speaks up and starts talking fast. "We're raising money to donate to their operations fund, and we thought it would be neat to bring two or three of the animals to our booth. That way, people can see how they are helping out by buying our lemonade. And maybe after seeing them in-person, someone might adopt one of the animals. If they don't get homes soon, they may have to be put to sleep. We'd keep the dogs enclosed, or on leashes, near our booth, so they wouldn't bother anyone."

Mrs. Jenkins puts her hand on her chin while she thinks. "I see."

"The dogs from the shelter are all very well-behaved," Carly continues. "I've worked with them for the past few months. I can guarantee they won't cause any trouble."

"That's quite a lofty promise, young lady," answers Mrs. Jenkins. "I'm a pet owner myself, and I don't think anyone can guarantee a dog's behavior. But I can clearly see how much you care for the animals. It's admirable what you're doing to find them good homes. Many of our Lemonade Day participants just sign on to make money for themselves."

"Actually, I'm thinking about giving all my money to the shelter," adds Carly. "I get an allowance from my parents to buy things that I want, and the animals need so much."

"You've sold me on the idea!" Mrs. Jenkins claps her hands. "Your team may bring three dogs from the shelter to Lemonade Day. But you must promise to keep them contained, or leashed at your booth, as you suggested. I'll put together a permission slip form for you and your mentor to sign, agreeing that you'll be fully responsible for the dogs and anything they do. Pick it up here at the office by tomorrow afternoon, and have your mentor turn it in when you set up at Lemonade Day."

"Thanks so much, Mrs. Jenkins!" Carly pumps her fist in the air.

The four of us leave the office, and Nathan high-fives Carly as soon as we step out the door.

"Dang, girl! If you don't become a veterinarian, you might be a lawyer one day," he compliments her.

"Sophie talked too; it wasn't just me," she says with a blush.

"You were the one who convinced Mrs. Jenkins to let us bring the dogs," Nathan insists.

"Great job, Carly!" parrots Cole.

Though what the boys are saying is true, I feel like a huge burrito is in my stomach. Carly could barely speak when Mrs. Jenkins first started listening to us. I got the conversation going.

"Wait a minute," says Carly. "With all the excitement of asking about the animals, I forgot to make copies of our fliers."

"Here's the folder with all the pictures." Cole hands it to her.

My cell phone buzzes, and I pull it out and look down at the message. "Mom's outside now, Cole," I say. "We better get going."

"I'll help you, Carly," say Nathan. "Afterward, we can hang a few of the fliers up around the school."

"Now everybody will see your awesome artwork," He looks down at Cole.

"I've had pictures up on the wall in my class before." Cole puffs out his chest.

"Good idea, Nathan, thanks!" Carly says, smiling brightly. "Chloe wanted to put some fliers up too. I'll slip copies in her locker and in your locker too, Sophie. See you guys later!"

"Yeah, see ya!" I answer, following behind as my little brother skips to the school entrance.

"See you, Cole!" calls Nathan.

"Bye, Nathan," I say.

He doesn't give me a backward glance.

CHAPTER 17

Finishing Touches

By Friday afternoon, we have all our marketing in place.

"Carly, Nathan, and I taped fliers all around the school this morning," Chloe checks off items on our to-do list on the ride to my house after school. "My mom and I ironed designs on tee shirts for all of us, using some extra shirts I had left over at my house from doing tie dye."

"Did you bring the tee shirts with you?" Carly leans over the car seat. "I'll bet they're super-cute."

"It better not be pink," Cole scrunches up his nose.

"You'll love it," assures Chloe. "My backpack's in the trunk, so I'll pass the shirts out at Sophie's house."

"What'cha reading?" Cole pulls on Nathan's sleeve.

He's had his nose in his science book the entire drive. I want to say something to him about yesterday, but I'm not sure how.

"Wow!" Carly heads straight to the lemonade stand as soon as we hop out of the SUV. "The pictures you showed us of the lemonade stand looked great, but it's even better in person."

"I can't believe you guys made this yourselves." Nathan rubs his hands across the smooth, painted surface and the white and yellow awning.

After it finished drying last weekend, Dad pulled our lemonade stand over to a side corner in the driveway. We've kept Bertram in the backyard all week to keep it safe.

"Wanna see our tee shirts?" Chloe unzips her backpack right after Mom pops the trunk. She pulls out a yellow shirt with a lemon design on it.

"Nice!" Nathan holds his shirt over his chest.

"Let's take a picture!" Chloe suggests.

"Say cheese!" Mom instructs. We all lean in behind the stand. "Can I get one more, in case someone's eyes are closed?"

"Hurry up, Mom!" Cole hops on one foot, "I gotta use the bathroom!"

"You kids have done a wonderful job putting everything together," Mom says once we're inside. "I'm sure your lemonade stand will be a success."

We wash up, have a quick snack, and start working. An hour later, our last-minute prep is in full swing. Mrs. Gentry and Alexis come by, and they're with us in the kitchen.

"Can you get some lemons out of the refrigerator, Cole?" I rub my sticky fingers on my white apron.

"Here ya go, Sis!" He opens the stainless-steel door, reaches into the crisper and throws me a couple.

A cake-scented candle burns on the kitchen table, and there's a stack of light blue file folders beside it. Mom and Mrs. Gentry sip coffee, while she puts finishing touches on Mrs. Gentry's business plan.

"The bank has got to accept this!" Mrs. Gentry smiles as she flips through the thick, typed-up report.

"I believe we've got everything covered." Mom nods her head in agreement. "Your business plan is reasonable, and your product is fantastic. Our appointment with the banker to see if they'll give you a loan is this Wednesday."

"You Washingtons are a true family of entrepreneurs." Mrs. Gentry turns to Mom. "You're a business consultant, your husband owns a dental practice, and your kids have their own lemonade stand."

"I'm a 'preneur too," Alexis pipes up. "I wanna help!"

She's stands on tiptoes by me at the stove, while I stir in cups of sugar in boiling water to make the lemonade syrup. Chloe and Nathan cut strawberries to freeze for our Berry Special recipe. On the opposite counter, Carly mixes flour, butter, sugar, spices, and chocolate chips for the cookies.

While we work, Cole hands out ingredients and video tapes us with my cell phone.

"How many strawberries have you cut?" he asks Nathan.

"It feels like infinity and beyond," Nathan answers with a laugh.

He's still barely spoken to me. Maybe I'll apologize before he goes home.

"Let me interview you, 'Lexie." Cole gestures to the smaller girl with his index finger.

"Be careful," I warn my little brother. "You better not drop my phone."

I pour some of the cooled down syrup into a drink dispenser and squeeze in fresh lemon juice. We'll keep all of the lemonade in the refrigerator overnight, so it'll be extra cold tomorrow.

"That's cool that your next-door-neighbor donated lemons from her lemon tree, Chloe." I slice another piece of the citrus fruit.

"Not having to buy lemons cuts our spending budget in half," Nathan speaks to me for the first time, since yesterday. "If we have as many people visiting our booth as we expect, we'll make plenty to donate to the shelter and have money left over."

Chloe sets down the strawberry she's hulling on a cutting board and joins me, Cole, and Alexis by the kitchen island. "Hey! I have a great idea to tell more people about our lemonade stand!"

CHAPTER 18

Viral Video

"Record us, Cole." Chloe stands in front of Alexis with her hands up.

"Come on, 'Lexie. Let's play Lemonade!" Chloe starts the hand clap game we taught Alexis a couple of weeks ago, and she joins in.

> *Lemonade (clap, clap, clap)*
> *Crunchy ice (clap, clap, clap)*
> *Sip it once (clap, clap, clap)*
> *Sip it twice (clap, clap, clap)*
> *Lemonade*
> *Crunchy Ice*
> *Sip it once*
> *Sip it twice*
> *Turn around*
> *Touch the ground*
> *Kick your partner out of town!*
> *Freeze!*

Chloe hops out of her freeze pose and looks into the camera. "Come see us at Xavier Academy's Lemonade Day event for refreshing lemonade, snacks, and plenty of fun! Some of our profits will go to help dogs and cats at Woodbridge Animal Shelter. Hope you'll join us tomorrow at Booth 10."

Cole stops recording, and I rush around the kitchen island to watch the video.

"That's so cute," says Carly.

"Great idea!" Nathan agrees.

"Look at me, Mamma!" Alexis points at the phone, and then bounces up and down.

"I'm posting this to my social media account!" Chloe clicks the send button.

"Wait a minute." Mom holds up her hand like a stop sign. "Did you get Mrs. Gentry's permission to put Alexis on the Internet?"

"It's fine," Mrs. Gentry answers. "I think it's wonderful that the kids are using technology to support a good cause."

"We already have twenty likes!" Chloe exclaims, five minutes later.

"Little 'Lexie is going viral!" I look at the numbers and laugh.

"Hmmm…" Mom cradles her face with her fingers. "I'd included Internet ads to Mrs. Gentry's business plan, but maybe we should make some videos to post to social media too."

"It smells wonderful in here!" Dad walks through the back door.

"Like a full-on bakery." He leans over the counter, where Carly stands with a rolling pin with the cookie dough.

"Don't get too excited, because all of these treats are for Lemonade Day." Mom walks over and kisses his cheek. "We're having pizza for dinner tonight."

"Yummo! Can we eat with the big kids, Mommy?" Alexis skips over to Mrs. Gentry.

"We're heading home, sweetpea, but yes, we can order pizza at our house tonight too."

"Thanks again for all the hard work on my business plan," she turns to Mom. "And good luck at Lemonade Day tomorrow, kids. Alexis and I will be by to sample some of your treats."

We finish up our prep work around six o'clock. The pizzas Mom ordered arrive just a few minutes later. It's good she bought three boxes because we're all starved.

"Slow down, son!" Dad warns as Cole shoves his third extra cheese slice in his mouth.

"Sorry, but it's sooo good." Cole flutters his eyelashes like he's in heaven, making everyone laugh.

"See you guys at the school at ten a.m. sharp," I walk Chloe and Carly to the door an hour later.

"And make sure to wear your tee shirts," Chloe reminds us, as her dad's gray sedan pulls into the driveway.

"Okay! See ya!" I wave when they walk outside.

"I can't wait for Lemonade Day, can you?" I turn to Nathan, once the girls are gone. Cole is outside feeding Bertram, and my parents are cleaning up in the kitchen.

"Everything so far has been a lot of fun," he says quietly.

"We have the best team!" I answer.

"You think so?" He tilts his head.

"Yeah, I do." I wring my hands. "Look, I don't know if you heard any of my conversation with Toby the other day, but...."

A horn honks outside, and Nathan turns around. "My dad's just pulled up. I better go."

"Wait, Nathan! About the other day!" I touch his shoulder.

"Don't worry about it," he answers. "I know you wanted Toby to be on the team."

"I don't know why I said what I did." I stare down at my feet. "I didn't mean any of that. I want you to be in our group."

"You've got a great way of showing it!" He glares. "You know, I felt really bad when I forgot about my science project and almost couldn't be on the team. And I went through some changes to move the date of my experiment, so I could help you guys. But that's okay. Lemonade Day is over tomorrow. You can spend the rest of your time with Toby."

"That's not what I want to do, Nathan." I bite my lip. "You're my friend too, and I'm happy to spend time with you."

"Alright sure." He shrugs my hand off his shoulders. "I gotta go. See you in the morning."

He strides down the pathway and hops in his dad's car without looking back.

As we get ready for bed, Cole's bouncing around like it's Christmas Eve, but I feel like I found a lump of coal in my stocking. No way did I want things to end up like this with Nathan.

"I hope things go well tomorrow," I say to Goldy before turning off my night light and climbing under my blanket. I toss and turn as I try to fall asleep.

CHAPTER 19

Tummy Trouble

"My stomach hurts." Cole stands over my bed holding his belly.

"Go back to bed," I grumble, pulling the covers over my head.

"I mean it." He shakes my shoulders. "I don't feel so good."

"You can't be sick! It's Lemonade Day." I snuggle deeper into my quilt. In my dream, I'm sitting under a sweet-smelling lemon tree, sipping a tall glass of Granny Washington's Berry Special.

"Mmmm…mmmm…mmmm." Bertram's loud, whining wakes me back up.

"What time is it?" I mumble. Besides the glow from my night light, it's black. "Why didn't you go to Mom and Dad's room?"

"The hall light is off. It hurts…." Cole groans again, sounding like an old man. "I'm gonna throw up!"

I feel like I've been squirted in the face with a water gun and sit up. "Not on my bed!" I cry.

"Come on! Let's go to the bathroom." I kick my heavy quilt off my legs, thud to the floor, and yank Cole's hand. We make it halfway down the hallway before Cole bends over and hurls.

"Ewww!" Vomit, with white chunks in it, flows out of his mouth like water from a faucet onto the shiny wooden floor. Cole slides to his knees when he's done.

"Get up!" Turning my head to the side, so I won't breathe in the stink, I help my brother to his feet. Bertram barks, and Dad opens his bedroom door and flicks on the hallway light.

"What're you kids doing out here?" He rubs his eyes. "It's three a.m."

"Cole got sick." I point at the mess.

"Oh my goodness!" Mom sticks her head out of the room. "It must have been the pizza."

My brother's stomach has to be completely empty, because enough came out of it to fill a sauce pan.

"I'm sorry I made a mess, Mommy." Cole wraps his arms around me tighter to keep from falling down.

"It's alright, sweetie," she answers, moving closer to us. "Let's get you washed up and back to bed."

Dad rushes past me on his way downstairs to fetch a bucket and some liquid cleaner. Mom guides Cole out of my arms and moves him to the bathroom for a bath.

"Bring some clean pajamas and underwear from your brother's room," she calls to me.

Bertram follows like a body guard while I walk into Cole's room.

"Oof!" I almost trip over a toy light saber to get to his chest of drawers and pull out his favorite Black Panther PJs.

"Thanks, dear." Mom takes the clean clothes from my hands and passes them to Cole. Wrapped in a fluffy, white bathrobe, he looks like he's not in pain anymore.

Within thirty minutes, the floor smells like pine cleaner, and we're all back in bed. Cole could barely hold his eyelids open by the time Mom helped him into his pajamas, but he seems to be feeling better. I'm happy that Bertram lays down nearby to keep a watch over him.

"Get some rest, Sophie." Dad pats my back before he tucks in Cole's cover. Satisfied that every thing's okay, I pad down to my room, flop onto the bed, and burrow back under the covers.

When I wake up at daylight, I forget about what happened with Cole for a second. Then I panic.

"What time is it?!" I glance at the clock on my nightstand. It's almost nine o'clock. We'd planned to get up extra early today to eat a big breakfast and load everything in the car. I don't smell bacon and eggs cooking. And usually, Bertram would have been in my room by now.

My chest tight, I go to use the restroom and see what's up. Cole's door is closed, and when I look in his room, he's in the bed snoring. Bertram is nowhere to be found.

"Mom! Dad! We've got to get going!" I rush down the staircase. "We're gonna be late for Lemonade Day!"

"Hold your horses, young lady." My father stops me as I stumble into the kitchen. "Everything's alright. I just finished loading up the supplies in the truck, and I was getting ready to wake you up."

"What are we eating for breakfast?" I look around the spotless kitchen. "Where's Mom?"

"Cole still seems weak from getting sick last night, so your mother's going to stay home with him," Dad answers. "She went to get some donuts for breakfast at the shop down the street, since we woke up late. I'll help your group out at Lemonade Day."

"But Mom's our mentor!" I cry. "She's supposed to be there to make sure we're doing things the right way."

"I know a little bit about business too." Dad puts his hands on my shoulders. "And from what I've seen, you kids have done a fantastic job getting things organized. I'll be there with you early-on, and if Cole feels better in the afternoon, Mom can bring him over to join us."

I ball my hands into fists.

"It's not fair!" I hunch over. "I'm so tired of Mom putting Cole first."

"They might come later," Dad soothes. "Let's see how he feels in a couple of hours. Now, I need you to get dressed so we won't be late to meet the team."

CHAPTER 20

Booth 10

"Sophie! Over here!" Chloe flags me down, after we pull into the school parking lot and step out. Since most of the paved area is blocked off for lemonade stands, Dad parks his SUV in the gravel.

My bestie reminds me of sunshine in her yellow tee shirt, with a lemon-colored barrette in her hair.

"Hey guys!" Carly runs up to us.

"Hi!" Chloe waves. "Did you see the views on our Lemonade Day video?"

"Wow! One thousand!" Carly exclaims.

With all the lemonade stands in place, it feels like a carnival in Xavier's parking lot. Pop music plays from speakers, and rainbow-colored balloons float above the school marquee. There are bouncy houses and a small petting zoo with sheep and goats on the soccer field.

A person in a costume that looks like a giant pitcher of lemonade leads a line dance. Mrs. Jenkins and parent volunteers rush around with clipboards, telling kids where to set up.

In the parking lot, half the Lemonade Day teams decorate card tables with festive, table cloths and banners on them. But the other four teams have full, built-out lemonade stands like ours.

"Can you girls carry these?" Dad pulls drink dispensers and a bag filled with cookies and napkins from the trunk.

"I'll bring the lemonade stand over," he says, while we fill our hands with supplies.

Our feet crunch on the gravel, as we make our way across the parking lot to space number ten. Holding my bag tightly, I'm careful not to crush any of the cookies inside.

"Check that out!" Chloe nods at a lemonade stand, directly across from our area, that's painted teal blue. The group's charity is a women's hospital, and pink, pacifiers and baby rattles decorate their awning.

The stand next to that one has a Hawaiian theme, with a grass skirt around the bottom. The team members wear Hawaiian shirts and have colorful leis wrapped around their necks.

"Where's your mom and Cole?" Chloe looks around.

"Cole got sick from eating too much pizza and threw up," I explain. "He was still in bed when we left. But they might be able to make it later."

"What a bummer!" says Chloe. "I know he hates to miss all the fun."

My face burns when I think about Mom sitting home with Cole feeding him soup instead of being our mentor like she promised.

"Anyone talked to Nathan?" Carly looks around. "I haven't seen him, either."

"I hope the pizza didn't make him sick too." I set down my bag. "What if he doesn't show up?"

"Yeah, we really need his help," says Carly. "Plus, he's doing our business plan. That's a big part of the judging. Without him, Lemonade Day might be a disaster."

"Here comes Ms. Vincent!" She glances toward the parking lot. The pet center director walks behind my father, with Lady, Fuzzy, and Maxine on leashes. Dad pulls our lemonade stand on a wheeled cart.

"This is fantastic!" says Ms. Vincent when my father removes the protective sheet from the white, painted stand.

"The kids did a wonderful job," Dad agrees. "I'm really proud of them. Let's get everything set up to be ready for customers."

I grab a basket filled with lemons to put on a front shelf. Chloe and Carly set out cookies, hand sanitizer, and our chalkboard sign with prices. Dad brings our coolers filled with the drinks, and we set napkins, plastic cups, and straws on one of the back shelves.

"Where should the animals be?" Ms. Vincent asks.

"Here on the side will be fine," says Dad.

Beside our stand, the director displays a poster board sign with the shelter's name and phone number on it. She sets a stack of fliers with information on pet adoption on top of the lemonade stand.

"Hey, Poochie!" Chloe scratches Lady on the head, and the chihuahua rubs its chin against her other hand.

Excited to be out in the sunshine around all the action, Fuzzy and Maxine wag their tails.

By ten thirty, our lemonade stand is ready for business. Nathan still hasn't shown up. I'm anxious as I look back at the parking lot again.

"Here comes Valentina!" Chloe spots our friend. Weaving through the crowd, Valentina looks like a fairy princess in a lavender satin dress that floats below her knees. A group of other girls in identical outfits, one in a long, purple gown, and some boys in tuxedos are on the soccer field.

"Hola!" she greets us in Spanish. "Your lemonade stand is fantastico! I definitely want to do this with you guys next year!"

"And you look beautiful, Valentina!" I admire her gown. "Why're you so dressed up?"

"It's my cousin's quinceañera today, remember?" she answers. "We're taking pictures this morning before the ceremony."

"Let's get a shot of us with you at our lemonade stand!" Chloe pulls her cell phone out. "Lean in, Carly."

"Photo bomb!" Someone jumps out as Chloe pushes the button.

"Get out of here, guys!" Carly frowns at Toby and one his friends from the basketball team.

Toby poses like a muscle man behind us.

"You know your picture looks better with me in it." He winks and then laughs.

"I thought you guys couldn't come to Lemonade Day because of your playoff practice," I say.

"Coach canceled it," he answers.

"We're short a couple of team members, could you help us out?" I ask.

"It's the weekend. I need to relax." He crosses his arms around his chest. "I don't have time to make lemonade."

"But we need you," I beg. "I thought you said you'd do all you could to help a friend."

"You know we're cool, but my Pops is picking me up in an hour," he shrugs. "I want to have some fun before my game."

"Customers are coming," Chloe steps in when I put my hands on my hips. "We need to get back to work."

"Come on, Jacob, let's go to the soccer field." Toby grabs his friend's arm. "We might come back to buy a drink from you ladies after we go to the bounce house." He gives us the peace sign.

I bite my lip as they walk away. Some friend!

"Thank goodness those two aren't on our Lemonade Day team," says Chloe, as Toby and his buddy bounce off. "They aren't dependable."

"It's starting to get hot." Valentina fans her face with her hand, "I hope we can finish up soon with the quinceañera pictures. We're waiting for one of the boys to get here."

"Same here," says Chloe. "It's almost time to start, and Nathan still hasn't shown."

"My mom and brother probably aren't coming either." I rub my toe on the ground.

Mrs. Jenkins walks to the center of the parking lot and waves her hands to get everyone's attention. "Lemonade Day will officially begin in ten minutes," she announces through a megaphone. "Team members, please make sure to have your business plans out and ready for the judges."

I chew on my fingernail and look around. Where's Nathan?

CHAPTER 21

To The Rescue

"There he is! That way!" Chloe points out Nathan's reddish-brown hair and glasses in the crowd.

Nathan and his dad roll over a large, popcorn machine, right behind a boy running in a black tuxedo.

"Looks like the rest of my group is here too," says Valentina. "I'd better head back! Hope you sell gallons of lemonade!"

She waves at Nathan and speed walks toward the soccer field.

"Sorry I'm late," Nathan slides his hands in his jean's pockets, once he makes it to our booth. "We had trouble loading up the popcorn machine."

"You're just in time." My dad comes over to help Mr. Jones set up. "The Lemonade Day committee says the event is about to start."

"Do you have our business plan?" asks Chloe.

"Sure, here it is." He pulls a report held in a clear report cover from his duffel bag. "And here's a strong box and change to take payments."

"This looks nice!" I rub my hand over the cover of the report he's typed up. He must have taken a few hours to get this together. "Thanks so much for all your hard work! I'm glad you're on our team, Nathan."

"You sure about that?" He squints. "I saw Toby leaving the booth."

"I wouldn't trade you for a bazillion of him." I shake my head.

"Actually, a bazillion is not a specific quantity." He scratches his head.

"You know what I mean!" I punch his arm.

"Let's pop some popcorn!" Chloe grabs a bag of kernels we unloaded earlier. "Show me what to do, Nathan."

They fill the container with dried kernels and oil, and Nathan's dad turns it on.

Within minutes, the air fills with the buttery, mixed with sweet, smell of popcorn.

"Yay! They have snacks *and* lemonade!" Alexis and Mrs. Gentry stroll to our lemonade stand.

"Hey, Lexie!" Chloe gives her a big smile.

"Those are the girls from the Lemonade Day video!" A boy around Cole's age and his father come up behind them and stare at Chloe and Alexis.

"You two are Internet sensations!" says Mrs. Gentry. "I'd like to try some of this famous lemonade and some popcorn too."

I pour a cup of regular lemonade and fill a bag with fluffy kernels to pass to them.

"That'll be three dollars," says Carly.

"Can you add on a Berry Special?" Mrs. Gentry pulls some extra bills out of her wallet. "I want to sample that too."

"Look at the doggies!" Alexis squats to get a better view of Lady, who is inside a portable enclosure Ms. Vincent brought.

"Arf! Arf!" The puppy wiggles its behind.

"She's my favorite too." Chloe joins Alexis near the cage.

The parking lot swells with Lemonade Day supporters. Hundreds of people buy drinks or visit the petting zoo and bouncy house. Mrs. Jenkins and a Lemonade Day judge sip from small cups and take notes at the stand across from ours. When they make it to us, I'll be sure to give them the Berry Special.

"Almost didn't find your booth in this crowd." Mom pushes to my side.

"Hey, Cole! How're you doing?" Nathan waves at my brother.

"Much better now." Cole says with a grin. "Mom made me eat an apple for breakfast. No more cheese for a while."

"Good idea!" Dad rubs his shoulder.

"How are things going?" Mom touches my shoulder.

"Fine." I move sideways to shrug her hand off.

"Is everything okay?" She frowns as I move away. "You kids did a great job putting the stand together."

"Even though we didn't have a mentor," I say under my breath.

"Sorry I'm late, Sis!" Cole steps up to me. "How can I help?"

"Let's pour some lemonade." I turn my back to my mother and pull him behind the lemonade stand.

A line forms that winds toward the animals. People wave and talk to the dogs, while they wait for their snacks and drinks. To keep things moving, Chloe fills the cups with ice, I pour drinks, and Carly takes the cash.

"How much money does a skunk have?" Cole entertains customers while he hands out filled cups. "One scent."

"Boy, you aren't even funny!" I pat him on the head.

"What you talkin' about?" He raises his eyebrow. "That girl and her grandpa just left me a tip."

"You guys are working like a well-oiled machine." Mom tries to talk to me again from the sidelines.

I pretend I don't hear her, but she gestures to Chloe to start pouring the drinks and pulls me to the side. "Need anything else from Dad's car? I left the permission slip we have to turn in to Mrs. Jenkins in his glove compartment, so I need to head back that way."

"If it was something for Cole you wouldn't have forgotten," I mutter.

"Don't be like that, Sophie." Mom bends down toward me. "You know that's not true."

"Yes, it is!" I hit my thigh with my hand. "As usual, you put him first."

"But your brother was sick," Mom says frowning. "I had to stay home with him."

"Dad could've done it." I poke out my lip. "He's a dentist. He knows how to take care of people. You always ignore me and do everything with Cole. You knew how important Lemonade Day was to me, and you didn't care. It's always all about Cole!"

A few of the customers look as I raise my voice.

Mom steps back. "I'm sorry I made you feel that way, sweetie. Maybe I could have come to set up instead of sending your father. I guess I just think of your brother as the baby of the family."

"Well, he's not." I point as Cole does a spin dance move while he's handing out cookies to customers.

My mother blinks. "You're right. I never meant to make you feel ignored. I'm so sorry, Sophie. How about we plan to do something together next weekend, just the two of us? Maybe get our nails done and have lunch. Would you like that?"

"Yes." I slowly nod.

"Great! We'll decide the details when we get home." She grabs my hand. "Come on, we need to attend to your business."

My shoulders relax, and I tighten my fingers around hers.

When I make it back around to help at the lemonade stand, Valentina returns with four boys from her quinceañera group.

"We'll take ten cups of regular lemonade and ten bags of popcorn."

"Whoa! That's twenty bucks!" Cole counts out the total on his fingers.

"Thanks so much for helping us out!" I high-five her.

"Anything for my girls, and this stuff is good!" Valentina gives the thumbs up sign as she hands over some bills.

By the time the Lemonade Day judges get to us, my heart pops in my chest like kernels from the popcorn machine.

"I wonder if she likes it," I whisper to Chloe, while Mrs. Jenkins takes a large drink of the Berry Special.

"Refreshing," the secretary says, patting the sides of her mouth with a yellow napkin. "And selling snacks was a great idea."

"This business plan is quite thorough." The other judge flips through the book Nathan put together. "Your team has done a wonderful job planning your business and running it. Kudos to you and your mentor."

"What's kudos mean?" whispers Alexis.

"I think good job," I answer.

We're the last booth to be rated for the judging, so Mrs. Jenkins and her partner walk to another spare table to count the scores. "We'll announce the winners shortly," she says.

A half hour later, the crowd has thinned out in the parking lot. Many of the people have migrated to the bouncy house and petting zoo areas. Chloe, Carly, and Alexis play with the dogs, while Ms. Vincent talks with Mrs. Gentry and a couple of other people about pet adoption.

I check to see how much lemonade we have in the cooler. The dispenser's almost empty.

I look around to see if the judges are ready to announce the team scores.

"Let's see how much money we've made." Nathan pulls bills from the strong box. "Over four hundred dollars!"

"Yay! We'll have plenty to pay you back, Mom," says Cole.

"About the money," Mom turns to us both. "I feel like I may have been a little hard on you kids. We have Bertram in and out of the garage all the time, and I probably shouldn't have stored Mrs. Gentry's candle containers there. I've decided to only make you pay back fifty dollars, for the replacement cost of Chloe's shoes."

"Thanks so much, Mom!" I hug her.

"You're the best mother ever!" Cole hugs from the other side.

"Hey, what about me? Don't I get a hug?" Dad raises his hands in the air. "I helped build your lemonade stand."

"You're the best dad in the world too!" I crush him into the group.

CHAPTER 22

Spending Money

"Our first place overall winner of this year's Lemonade Day is booth number five!" Mrs. Jenkins finally announces. The team with the Hawaiian-themed stand jumps around and cheers.

"First place for best tasting lemonade goes to booth ten's Berry Special recipe," says the other judge when the crowd dies down. "This team also wins second place overall for lemonade stand décor and design."

"Way to go, Sophie!" Chloe bumps me with her hips.

Nathan raises a cup filled with lemonade to me in a toast.

"I knew we could do it, once you figured out the difference between sugar and salt," Cole jokes.

"This turned out to be a wonderful day!" says Mom, as we pack up our remaining supplies.

"I'm so happy that Cole got over being sick." I smile as I grab a bag of leftover lemons.

"That extra rest did him good." Dad points at my little brother dancing with the Lemonade Day mascot.

"I wasn't expecting much when you signed up last minute," Mrs. Jenkins stops by our stand before going home. "But you kids did an excellent job. Congratulations on an outstanding performance."

"Thanks for letting us sign up, Mrs. Jenkins," I answer. "We had a lot of fun."

Nathan does a final count of our money from the strong box and writes the total on his notebook.

"We earned over five hundred dollars!" Chloe does a happy dance.

"That's one hundred dollars each!" Cole points at each of us to get the division right.

"Make that eighty dollars each," says Nathan. "Remember that we've giving twenty percent of our earnings to the animal shelter."

"And we have to give forty dollars to the sponsor to pay for the popcorn, berries, sugar and other supplies we bought." I add.

"Yeah, I forgot about that. Make that seventy-two dollars each," he says after doing some calculations in his head.

"I'm donating *all* my money to Woodbridge," says Carly.

"You're getting a whole lotta dog food." Cole peers at Fuzzy and Maxine tied up to a nearby post. Thinking my brother wants to play, Fuzzy jumps up on his leg.

"Down boy." My brother brushes him off. "I don't want Bertram to smell you on me. He's my number one dog."

"Hey, where's that teeny one?" Cole looks around for Lady. "Don't tell me it got loose."

"Lady's coming with us!" Alexis carries the dog on her shoulders in a messenger bag.

"So, your daughter finally broke you down." Mom turns to Mrs. Gentry.

"She did," Mrs. Gentry answers with a laugh. "And Lady is so cute, she melted my heart too."

"All three of our sweeties have found new homes." Ms. Vincent clasps her hand happily. "Two people are picking Fuzzy and Maxine up on Monday. I showed videos of the other pets on my electronic tablet throughout the event, and a few other folks have promised to visit the center to consider adopting them. This Lemonade Day event was phenomenal for us all."

"Lucky!" Chloe says to Alexis. "I wanted to adopt Lady. I may still get that doggy sweater as a housewarming gift for her when I go to the mall next weekend."

"Leave it to you to get a dog an outfit," teases Nathan.

"You'd probably clock her speed with your radar gun." I hit his ribs lightly with my elbow. "Seriously, thank you for being on our team and for being my friend."

"I had fun working with you guys too," says Nathan. "Thanks."

He and his dad take off, and we wait with Chloe and Carly until their parents come to pick them up.

"See you on Monday, guys!" I wave as they walk off.

"See ya, Sophie!"

I feel like dancing like the Lemonade Day mascot when we load the last of the things into Dad's SUV. We made more than enough money to pay back our debt to Mom and for my brother and I to be able to buy her a nice birthday gift. Plus, we had a lot of fun doing it.

On the drive home, I think about all the ups and downs of the past two weeks and remember what Mom said in the garage: "When life gives you lemons, make lemonade."

My friends and I made our own lemonade, and it was sweeter than Granny's Berry Special.

Dear Reader:

Thank you for reading *Sophie Washington: Lemonade Day*. I hope you liked it. If you enjoyed the book, I'd be grateful if you post a short review on Amazon. Your feedback really makes a difference and helps others learn about my books. I appreciate your support!

Tonya Duncan Ellis

P.S. Please visit my website at tonyaduncanellis.com to see videos about Sophie and learn about upcoming books (I sometimes give away freebies!). You can also join Sophie's Club to get updates about my new releases and get a **FREE** gift.

GRANNY WASHINGTON'S "BERRY SPECIAL" LEMONADE

"Berry Special" lemonade was a bestseller at Sophie and friends' lemonade stand. Try out the recipe to make this refreshing drink yourself!

Ingredients

1 cup lemon juice
1 cup frozen berries (strawberries, blackberries, raspberries, blueberries)
1 cup simple syrup
3 cups cold water

Instructions

- Place berries in an ice cube tray, cover with water and freeze overnight.
- Create simple syrup. Combine equal parts, granulated sugar and water (about one cup each) and boil until sugar dissolves. Let cool.
- Cut lemons in half and squeeze out juice, until you have one cup of lemon juice.
- Slice two lemons to add to a pitcher. Pour in lemon juice and sugar water. Stir to combine and refrigerate until chilled.
- Add berry cubes to the pitcher, stir and serve.

Source: @MomOnTimeout

LEMONADE DAY FACTS

Lemonade Day started when founder, Michael Holthouse's daughter, Lissa, wanted to add a turtle to her pet collection. With so many pets already in the house, Michael said no. Not accepting his answer, Lissa decided she would start a lemonade stand to raise money to buy her own turtle and asked her dad for help. The rest, as they say, is history, and Lemonade Day was born.

Today, Lemonade Day teaches kids across North America how to start and operate their own business, so they can achieve their personal goals and fulfill their own dreams.

Below are other fun facts about lemonade and Lemonade Day:

- Since 2007, Lemonade Day has reached more than one million youth in sixty cities across the United States and Canada. In 2016 alone, more than 101,000 kids participated.
- On average, Lemonade Day kids make a profit of $168.08 at their lemonade stand and see their profits increase each year they participate in the program.

- 73% of Lemonade Day participants share a portion of their profit by giving back to their communities. Some groups that benefit from their generosity include: animal shelters, religious and youth organizations, hospitals, medical research funds, food banks, and more.
- 79% of Lemonade Day participants save a portion of their profits, with 20% of them opening their own savings account.
- The beverage lemonade originated in 500 AD and was invented by the Egyptians when they mixed lemon juice with sugar to make a beverage they called *qatarmizat*.
- The "ade" in lemonade means the product is not 100 percent juice.
- California and Arizona produce 95% of the entire U.S. lemon crop.
- A single lemon tree can produce up to 500 or 600 pounds of lemons in just one year.
- The earliest documented lemonade stands were in 1873 in Brooklyn and were run out of streetcars.

Source: @Lemonadeday.org

Books by
Tonya Duncan Ellis

For information on all Tonya Duncan Ellis books about Sophie and her friends

Check out the following pages!

You'll find:

* Blurbs about the other exciting books in the Sophie Washington series.

Sophie Washington
Queen of the Bee

Sign up for the spelling bee?
No way!

If there's one thing ten-year-old Texan Sophie Washington is good at, it's spelling. She's earned straight one-hundreds on all her spelling tests to prove it. Her parents want her to compete in the Xavier Academy spelling bee, but Sophie wishes they would buzz off.

Her life in the Houston suburbs is full of adventures, and she doesn't want to slow down the action. Where else can you chase wild hogs out of your yard, ride a bucking sheep or spy an eight-foot-long alligator during a bike ride through the neighborhood? Studying spelling words seems as fun as getting stung by a hornet, in comparison.

That's until her irritating classmate, Nathan Jones, challenges her. There's no way she can let Mr. Know-it-All win. Studying is hard when you have a pesky younger brother and a busy social calendar. Can Sophie ignore the distractions and become Queen of the Bee?

Sophie Washington
The Snitch

There's nothing worse than being a tattletale...

That's what ten-year-old Sophie Washington thinks until she runs into Lanie Mitchell, a new girl at school. Lanie pushes Sophie and her friends around at their lockers and even takes their lunch money.

If they tell, they are scared the other kids in their class will call them snitches and won't be their friends. And when you're in the fifth grade, nothing seems worse than that. Excitement at home keeps Sophie's mind off the trouble with Lanie.

She takes a fishing trip to the Gulf of Mexico with her parents and little brother, Cole, and discovers a mysterious creature in the attic above her room. For a while, Sophie is able to keep her parents from knowing what is going on at school. But Lanie's bullying goes too far, and a classmate gets seriously hurt. Sophie needs to make a decision. Should she stand up to the bully or become a snitch?

Sophie Washington
Things You Didn't Know
About Sophie

Oh, the tangled web we weave...

Sixth grader Sophie Washington thought she had life figured out when she was younger, but this school year everything changed. She feels like an outsider because she's the only one in her class without a cell phone, and her crush, new kid Toby Johnson, has been calling her best friend Chloe. To fit in, Sophie changes who she is. Her plan to become popular works for a while, and she and Toby start to become friends.

Between the boy drama, Sophie takes a whirlwind class field trip to Austin, Texas, where she visits the state museum, eats Tex-Mex food, and has a wild ride on a kayak. Back at home, Sophie fights off buzzards from her family's roof, dissects frogs in science class, and has fun at her little brother Cole's basketball tournament.

Things get more complicated when Sophie "borrows" a cell phone and gets caught. If her parents make her tell the truth what will her friends think? Turns out Toby has also been hiding something, and Sophie discovers the best way to make true friends is to be yourself.

Sophie Washington
The Gamer

40 Days Without Video Games? Oh No!

Sixth-grader Sophie Washington and her friends are back with an interesting book about having fun with video games while keeping balance. It's almost Easter, and Sophie and her family get ready to start fasts for Lent with their church, where they give up doing something for forty days that may not be good for them. Her parents urge Sophie to stop tattling so much and encourage her second-grade brother, Cole, to give up something he loves most—playing video games. The kids agree to the challenge but how long can they keep it up? Soon after Lent begins, Cole starts sneaking to play his video games. Things start to get out of control when he loses a school electronic tablet he checked out without his parents' permission and comes to his sister for help. Should Sophie break her promise and tattle on him?

Sophie Washington Hurricane

#Sophie Strong

A hurricane's coming, and eleven-year-old Sophie Washington's typical middle school life in the Houston, Texas suburbs is about to make a major change. One day she's teasing her little brother,

Cole, dodging classmate Nathan Jones' wayward science lab frog and complaining about "braggamuffin" cheerleader Valentina Martinez, and the next, she and her family are fleeing for their lives to avoid dangerous flood waters. Finding a place to stay isn't easy during the disaster, and the Washington's get some surprise visitors when they finally do locate shelter. To add to the trouble, three members of the Washington family go missing during the storm, and new friends lose their home. In the middle of it all, Sophie learns to be grateful for what she has and that she is stronger than she ever imagined.

Sophie Washington
Mission: Costa Rica

Welcome to the Jungle

Sixth grader Sophie Washington, her good friends, Chloe and Valentina, and her parents and brother, Cole, are in for a week of adventure when her father signs them up for a spring break mission trip to Costa Rica. Sophie has dreams of lazing on the beach under palm trees, but these are squashed quicker than an underfoot banana once they arrive in the rainforest and are put to work, hauling buckets of water, painting, and cooking. Near the hut they sleep in, the girls fight off wayward iguanas and howler monkeys, and nightly visits from a surprise "guest" make it hard for them to get much rest after their work is done.

A wrong turn in the jungle midway through the week makes Sophie wish she could leave South America and join another classmate who is doing a spring break vacation in Disney World.

Between the daily chores the family has fun times zip lining through the rainforest and taking an exciting river cruise in crocodile-filled waters. Sophie meets new friends during the mission week who show her a different side of life, and by the end of the trip she starts to see Costa Rica as a home away from home.

Sophie Washington
Secret Santa

Santa Claus is Coming to Town

Christmas is three weeks away and a mysterious "Santa" has been mailing presents to sixth grader Sophie Washington. There is no secret Santa gift exchange going on at her school, so she can't imagine who it could be. Sophie's best friends, Chloe, Valentina, and Mariama guess the gift giver is either Nathan Jones or Toby Johnson, two boys in Sophie's class who have liked her in the past, but she's not so sure. While trying to uncover the mystery, Sophie gets into the holiday spirit, making gingerbread houses with her family, helping to decorate her house, and having a hilarious ice skating party with her friends. Snow comes to Houston for the first time in eight years, and the city feels even more like a winter wonderland. Between the fun, Sophie uncovers clues to find her secret Santa and the final reveal is bigger than any package she's opened on Christmas morning. It's a holiday surprise she'll never forget!

Sophie Washington
Code One

Girl Power!

Xavier Academy is having a computer coding competition with a huge cash prize! Sixth grader Sophie Washington and her friend Chloe can't wait to enter with their other classmates, Nathan and Toby. The only problem is that the boys don't think the girls are smart enough for their team and have already asked two other kids to work with them. Determined to beat the boys, Sophie and Chloe join forces with classmates Mariama, Valentina, and "brainiac," Rani Patel, to form their own all-girl team called "Code One." Computer coding isn't easy, and the young ladies get more than they bargain for when hilarious mishaps stand in their way. It's girls versus boys in the computer coding competition as Sophie and her friends work day and night to prove that anything boys can do girls can do better!

Sophie Washington
Mismatch

Watch out Venus and Serena, Sophie Washington just joined the tennis team, and she's on her way to becoming queen of the court!

That is until her coach matches her with class oddball, Mackenzie Clark, and the drama really begins....Mackenzie refuses to talk to Sophie or learn the secret handshake she made up. Sophie just can't figure her out. Then Mackenzie starts skipping practice, and gets sick at school, and Sophie realizes that there's more to her doubles partner than meets the eye. Can Sophie make things right with Mackenzie before their first big game, or is their partnership a complete mismatch?

Sophie Washington
My BFF

You've Got A Friend In Me

Sophie and Chloe have been best friends since they met in kindergarten. They get along like chips and salsa and do everything together from playing tennis to cheering on the school cheer squad. Lately, Chloe's been leaving Sophie out, and she doesn't know why. Sophie does everything she can to make her best friend happy, but it's not working. Then Chloe asks Sophie to fib to a teacher to help her out and she learns the true meaning of friendship.

Sophie Washington
Class Retreat

There is no such thing as Big Foot! Or is there?

Sophie Washington and her classmates are on their way to Camp Glowing Spring for a class retreat. It'll be two full days of swimming, eating s'mores around a campfire, tug-of-war, archery, and more! Sophie's been looking forward to the trip all school year and can't wait to spend extra time with her friends. It will also be great to get away from her bratty younger brother, Cole, and his constant stories about Big Foot. If Cole warns her about what to do if she sees the hairy ape man on the retreat one more time, she'll put in ear plugs. Everybody knows Big Foot is a hoax!

Once the kids arrive at the retreat site things are as exciting as Sophie imagined. She has fun exploring nature with her besties, Chloe, Valentina, Toby, Nathan, and Mariama, and meeting new friends too. Then the kids see a giant footprint during a nature hike in the woods and the adventure really begins!

About the Author

Tonya Duncan Ellis is author of the Sophie Washington book series that includes: *Queen of the Bee, The Snitch, Things You Didn't Know About Sophie, The Gamer, Hurricane, Mission: Costa Rica, Secret Santa, Code One, Mismatch, My BFF, Class Retreat,* and *Lemonade Day.* When she's not writing, she enjoys reading, swimming, biking and travel. Tonya lives in Houston, TX with her husband and three children.

Made in the USA
Monee, IL
07 April 2022